About the author

Peter Milwain is a chartered accountant. He is married, has two children and lives in Scotland. This is his first novel.

The Honest Accountant

Peter Milwain

First Published in 2006 by Solway Publishing Limited

ISBN 0 9554274 0 1
ISBN 978 0 9554274 0 4

Solway Publishing Limited
Broadchapel House
Lochmaben
Dumfriesshire
DG11 1RL

CHAPTER 1

(FRIDAY 18TH APRIL 1997)

BLAIR SEEN AS KOHL PUPPET IN TORY AD
LORD SUTCH QUITS POLL TO LOOK AFTER MOTHER
CHIRAC PONDERS SNAP ELECTION TO SAVE EMU

Platt liked having lunch at his desk. No need for painful small talk or lumbering waiters, no need for time wasting. It was more efficient. Besides, it was the only chance he got to read the FT in comfort. Reading it on the tube was just too much hassle. Some folk could wrap themselves around the steel poles in the centre of the carriages whilst juggling newspapers and briefcases, he couldn't.

Platt read the FT in the same way every day. UK corporates, US corporates, the equity prices. He liked method, procedure and order. He noted that Rio Tinto were up ten pence and that his other holdings, ICI, GEC and Marks and Spencer were flat, still, he relished the prospect of calculating his capital gains this year. Like most accountants Platt was risk averse. Investments were always Blue Chip defensive stocks, solid and dependable, unspectacular, never unsafe.

He finished his ploughman's sandwich, neatly quartered the paper, and slotted it into the outside flap of his briefcase. He gently and meticulously brushed the crumbs from the Boardroom table into his hand and tipped them into the bin. He then opened the file at the place he had marked with a post-it before lunch and began to work.

Keith Platt was an auditor's auditor. He liked the perfect symmetry of the balance sheet where everything had to have its place. Every penny in, and every penny out, all had to be accounted for - nothing missed, nothing left out, no softness, no flexibility, just hard, incontrovertible numbers.

Platt had been with Blake and Lander, one of the so called Big 5 firms since he had graduated, and he was fast tracking to partnership. Senior manager next year was realistic, then partner four or even three years after that. Partner, that was where the real money was. Platt had heard that the starting rate for a junior partner was 200k, not bad for a Yorkshire lad from Goole Comprehensive. He thought of the residents of Humber View Close where his parents lived, and quickly calculated that it was unlikely that the combined income of the ten households that made up the cul-de-sac would top even £150k. Thinking of Humber View Close and how he had escaped it always gave Platt a warm glow.

Since he had arrived in London he had worked religiously on his accent and successfully softened his Yorkshire vowels, which were now difficult to detect when Platt talked in general conversation, and obliterated entirely if he talked on the phone or to partners. Indeed after six years of careful study and observation Platt felt that he could pass for any Surrey or Hampshire Lifer, just like the rest of them.

The Boardroom of Platt's client was on the top floor of Connaught House which was at No 2 Connaught Lane. The room was glassed on three sides, the fourth wall being the exposed brick of the building itself. Next door Platt could see the Managing Director of Everyman Credit, Jonathan Bridger, reclining at an angle of forty-five degrees in his huge leather chair, feet on desk, bellowing down the phone. Platt could hear the Scotsman through the glass partition and he soon guessed he was talking to his boss, Peter Grey.

'For fuck's sake Peter, how can I write more business if you don't give me any bloody money?'

Platt caught the eye of Bridger's secretary, June Paterson, as she turned slightly towards her MD and smiled.

'Ever been on the receiving end of one of Jon's verbal barrages June?' asked the auditor.

'Never Keith, you know what he's like with his staff, nice as nine pence, never shouts or bawls, and always says please.'

She turned back to her desk and switched on her desk lamp. This had the effect of making the glass partition between herself and Platt partially reflective, enabling the auditor to surreptitiously study himself. He was dressed in the uniform of the City Accountant; blue suit with thick chalk stripes, light blue shirt and mauve tie. His cufflinks were silver and his black lace-up shoes were highly polished. On the Boardroom table he could see the Firm's black standard issue pilot bag, with the distinctive B&L logo emblazoned in gold on the front flap. Inside the bag were his tools of trade, the auditors' tools of trade. Six incomplete audit files, business cards, pens, audit paper and the obligatory calculator. He looked more closely at himself and thought that despite his thinning brown hair he was ageing well. At the beginning of his career he had often thought that because of his average height and slight build, he lacked the necessary gravitas to progress in the firm, but since then he had learnt to compose himself, and walk a little taller than his five foot ten inches belied.

Having decided that it had been bright enough after all, Mrs Paterson switched off her lamp and Platt's reflection disappeared from the partition. He was mildly irritated that the secretary had ended his affectionate self-appraisal and he looked at her again. She had been quite prickly towards him since he had arrived at Everyman despite his best efforts to be accommodating. Perhaps she had detected a hint of insincerity in his attentiveness to her, though Platt had always been careful to guard against giving off signals which might betray his arrogance.

Platt looked around the rest of the third floor. The staff were seated in two large rectangles. The largest rectangle had its longest side running parallel to the windows at the far end of the room, farthest away from where Platt sat. This rectangle was where the thirty odd underwriters sat, day in day out assessing the creditworthiness of Everyman's customers. The smaller rectangle, which was within earshot of Platt, was where the four customer services officers were. It was their job to deal, slowly, with borrowers who had missed a payment, and who had realised that by adding together the charges and penalties which Everyman hid in its loan agreements, they were in fact paying interest at a usurious rate of around sixty per cent. Platt could hear Tod Parker, whom he had interviewed during the audit, talking to a distressed borrower.

'I'm sorry Mr Dean,' said Parker. 'But it does state quite clearly in the loan agreement at paragraph 46.5, that a late payment will incur a penalty charge of forty pounds.'

Platt could see Parker begin to doodle on his A4 pad as Mr Dean no doubt sought to explain why those contractual terms did not apply to him.

'Yes that's right Mr Dean,' continued Parker. 'The penalty charge is added onto the loan amount, plus there's the additional interest which we have to levy on the interest which hasn't been paid on time. And the interest on the penalty charge, plus of course the interest which is accruing on the loan itself. That's why you still have £3,760 outstanding.'

Platt felt a brief flicker of sympathy for Mr Dean. Some of the calculations used and the terms employed by Everyman were hard enough for him, a chartered accountant, to understand, never mind the likes of poor Mr Dean. He thought about the profile of Mr Dean and others like him who were specifically targeted by Everyman. Typically employed in northern manufacturing with a dependent family and living in rented accommodation, customers like Mr Dean would sign up for a loan in October or November, just before Christmas. These were the sort of loans which were advertised on pages 30-40 of the tabloid press, or on the pages of Teletext under enticing banners such as, 'Solve all your debt problems in one, call Everyman Credit now!' Platt knew that for most customers Everyman rarely provided a solution to anything. Indeed the Company was renowned in the industry for its ruthless debt collection procedures and liberal use of the bailiffs. Perhaps this had been why Everyman's parent, Southern and London Bank, had decided to sell out to the

United and Caledonian after 220 years. And might explain why Bridger was arguing so much with his outgoing bosses.

The thought of the takeover prompted Platt to turn quickly to his file. If things went wrong post-takeover, pissed off purchasers always looked more closely at the last set of figures audited under the old regime. Although Everyman was only a small part of Southern, and hardly material, nobody was going to use Platt as a scapegoat, no one was going to thwart his partnership ambitions. The responsibility for the audit, of course, lay with the audit partner. But Platt had heard what had happened after other Blake and Lander fuck ups. Partners were never sacked because they couldn't be sacked. They were legal partners. And besides to sack, demote, or sideline a partner who had fucked up would smack of an admission of negligence. No, it was always the audit manager who got the bullet. Platt thought of his current boss Silas Craven, and wondered when he was likely to show up to review the files.

'Really Keith, you're not still working on those bloody provisions. I've told you before that once the Reds have been in for six months, unemployment will go through the roof and all the muppets who borrow from us will default.'

Platt had been so deep in thought that he hadn't seen Bridger come into the Boardroom and stand behind him.

Bridger moved to face Platt then continued. 'Then they'll introduce a law which lets defaulters off their debts. Just because they've lost their job, or their wife's died, or some other bleedin heart nonsense. That's it, Blair's Bleedin Heart Brigade we should call em, or even Bleedin Heart Red Brigade.' He chuckled at his own humour and Platt responded with a plastic smile.

'That's a typically pessimistic banker's view Jonathan. Anyway they've said they'll stick to the Tory's spending plans for two years, or is it three?'

'Don't you believe a word of it. You're too young to remember the misgovernment of the 70s, when Sunny Jim Callaghan and the rest of his clowns couldn't organise a piss up in a brewery. They may call themselves New Labour, but they haven't changed.'

Bridger sidled round from behind Platt to the other side of the Boardroom table in front of him.

'Change of Government or not,' said Platt with a provoking smile. 'A cynic might say that Everyman's provisions enabled you to hit budget plus ten percent again, just like you did last year and the previous five years, in fact every year since you took over here. It's almost as if you don't want the Boys at Group to set you a higher target, say budget plus twenty percent.'

'What a creative mind you've got for an auditor,' replied Bridger, in a mock hurt tone. 'It's almost as if you're accusing me of fiddling the books. You and I both know that the level of provisions is very judgemental. The previous audit managers from your firm never seemed to have any trouble with it.' Platt was not sure why that last remark made him feel defensive but it did. Was Bridger having a general swipe at auditors or just having a go at B&L?

'Come off it Jon,' replied Platt firmly, 'provisions are made and released in line with profits, just so the bottom line can look nice and smooth.'

Bridger roared with laughter. 'You'll never make partner with that sort of comment,' he said. 'The level of provisions *must* be right in this Company because they're signed off by the auditors.'

Platt realized he couldn't defend his position and was relieved when Bridger changed tack slightly when he continued.

'There's your boss taking home, what, say £400k a year, and for what, signing off the odd audit report. Christ, a monkey could do that. And here's me, 102 staff reporting to me, assets worth £400m, that's real responsibility, and for what, £70k a year and some worthless share options. I need that bonus.' Bridger walked towards the door. 'Other than the provisions, anything else that I should be worried about?'

'Just a bit of detail on that rebate we discussed.'

'Oh yes. I'll have a solution to that for you tomorrow.'

He left the room and Platt looked at him whilst he was

departing. Platt liked Bridger. He had a ready smile, an inventory of one-liners that most comics could only dream of, and the ability to produce a deep, natural sounding belly laugh even after the weakest of jokes. In short he was a born salesman and an able executive who'd turned Everyman around from near insolvency during the recession to solid profitability. Platt knew though that he'd had enough. Despite the swagger and confidence he was a man on the way out. Commuting down from his Kelso home on a Monday and returning north of the border on a Friday already qualified him as a part-timer. Everyman had been his personal fiefdom for seven years but now he had done all he could with it. Platt likened him to an early twentieth century Ottoman Pasha, who now faced an uncertain future after the overthrow of the Sultans on the Southern Board. United and Caledonian had their own finance house, with its own MD, which meant that Bridger was likely to be one of the 'synergies' dreamt up by United's advisors when they had made the bid. He looked around the entire top floor. Did Bridger's staff also realise that they too had been classified as synergies?

Platt turned back to his file and worked solidly until seven. As it was a Friday and as Sally was expected at the flat later that night he decided to treat himself to an early finish. He looked around the office and realised that he was the only person there. The night lighting had already come on and apart from the Boardroom the only other source of light came from the window of the lift at the far end of the room, which, because the lift was on the top floor, acted as a kind of beacon showing Platt the way home.

He meticulously wrote Monday's 'To Do' list and underlined the first item '£7m rebate,' then neatly placed the list at the front of the open file which he flipped shut and locked in the cupboard in the corner of the room. He put on his jacket and overcoat and picked up his laptop which unusually fit first time into the correct compartment of the carrying case. He switched off the Boardroom lights, which instantly enhanced the brightness from the lift, and left the room. As Platt approached he was momentarily disorientated as the room plunged into darkness, someone had called the lift from below. As there was only one lift, he pressed the call button and waited.

He was surprised that the lift didn't come immediately. The button was still illuminated in the call position, and as there was no sign of it coming, he set off down the stairs. The stairs circled the lift as they descended to the ground floor, and when he drew near the landing on the second floor, he heard the lift's motor start in response to the request he had made a few moments before. Continuing his descent, he reached the first floor landing at the same time as the lift. This enabled him to glance at the small window in the lift door as it sped past. The window on the outer door was only parallel with the inner door window for a split second, so Platt only caught a brief glimpse of the man inside.

The man looked directly at Platt and appeared to recognise him though Platt was certain he had never met the man before. The man looked away quickly as if caught in the act like a naughty child. Platt felt uneasy.

He reached the foyer of the building and saw that Jim, the security guard, wasn't there. Platt could smell cigarette smoke and see the half-completed Sun crossword on Jim's desk.

'Hello Jim…' he said nervously. He heard the lift stop at the third floor. Jim often had a habit of wandering off and had previously been disciplined by Bridger for deserting his post once too often. Platt stepped out of the building and looked up and down Connaught Lane. To his left he could see the traffic on Buckingham Palace Road and to his right, at the end of the street past the multi-storey car park, he could see the lights of the Duke of Connaught pub.

Platt jumped as he heard a shuffling noise at his back.

'Didn't mean to frighten you Keith,' said Jim, with a condescending look. 'Call of nature you know.'

'Has anyone odd gone into the building in the last few minutes?' asked Platt hurriedly.

'Just those Albanian cleaners,' replied Jim. 'They're all bloody odd looking.' Any non-Anglo-Saxon foreigner was always Albanian to Jim.

'I thought there was someone a bit odd in the lift just now,' said Platt, feeling a little foolish. 'Maybe I was mistaken.'

'Probably that one with the skin-head. I'll call Len down to watch the desk and I'll pop up to have a look.'

As Platt turned right into the Lane and bid Jim goodnight, he wondered how handy Jim would be against a determined intruder. Obese, sixty plus, and wheezing like a miner. He typified the ex-servicemen gone to seed who topped up their paltry pensions with night shift security work. Platt chuckled to himself as he thought of Jim's backup, Len, or Limping Len as the girls in Accounts called him - who was just as fat and unfit as Jim, but a little less mobile. The thought of that pair successfully tackling an intruder was risible. Jim was probably right though, Platt was being paranoid.

He crossed to the other side of the Lane and walked along the road by the side of the multi-storey car park wall. Given that the wall was ten feet high, he had little room for manoeuvre when the car hit him from behind. Trapped between the wall and the car, Platt died instantly.

CHAPTER 2

(SATURDAY 19TH APRIL 1997)

HOWE ATTACKS DAMAGING TORY ADVERT
GERMANS SEE PUPPET PLOY AS PITIFUL
GOLDSMITH TV DEMAND IS REJECTED BY COURT

Mackay never had been a morning person. He just didn't like getting out of bed. He preferred to ease himself into the day; letting the morning gradually wash over him until eventually he was completely immersed in it. A Saturday morning was no different. Just for a change he had gone down to The George last night with Ed, and, just for a change they had both had ten pints of strong lager, and, just for a change they had waxed lyrical about why they were in the George, by themselves, on yet another Friday night.

Mackay's hangover was full blown and he felt its kick as he stumbled out of bed and reached down for yesterday's clothes. He went down to the kitchen and noticed that his other flatmate, Atif, had already eaten, so instinctively Mackay reached for the grill. Of course the beauty of sharing a flat with a not very devout Muslim, like Atif, was that he never really got pissed, and so could always be relied on to cook himself too much breakfast. Consequently Mackay gulped down the four fat sausages that were on the grill pan, and after shaving and showering, pulled on his beige chinos, blue striped shirt and blue blazer, his election costume.

Given that he was to spend the day canvassing, he thought it prudent to scan over the morning's headlines, so he switched on the small Daewoo TV in the kitchen and looked for the remote control. Having found it, he brought up the Ceefax news pages.

Mackay scanned the headlines then read no further. The desired 'Poll shows late swing to Government' unsurprisingly, was not there. God he'd had his fill of New Labour spin and sycophantic leftist reporting by the BBC. Mackay chuckled as he thought of the advert depicting Tony Blair as a ventriloquist's dummy on Chancellor Kohl's knee. When the Prime Minister's ship had all but sunk who could blame him for having a bit of fun.

Mackay was the last canvasser to arrive at the Edwardian terrace in Balfour Street which was shared by the Barnes and West Putney Conservative Party (ground floor) and the Tanning Shop (first floor). He found Annabel Mylner sitting alone in the agent's room, with one leg on the floor, the other hooked around the edge of the desk, and her skirt hitched high up her thigh. Mackay gave her a quick sexual appraisal. He noted the firm legs, long jet black hair and considerable breasts straining against her black polo shirt. She was aware of his presence but took no action to adjust her position until he rounded the desk and stood about four feet in front of her. She shifted her backside slightly and grounded her semi-elevated leg.

'You're here then,' she said. 'The rest have already gone, you've got the Cresswell Estate again.'

Mackay tried to hold her gaze but she was just too attractive. She had very large brown Audrey Hepburn eyes but her face was fuller and her lips thicker. There was plenty of Annabel to get hold of and snuggle in to, and as she spun round to get some papers from the far side of the desk, Mackay wondered what the consequences would be, if he simply reached out and touched her arse. It might be worth a slap, but it was not worth jeopardizing his slim chances of going any further with her, which was after all, the whole point of being here in the first place. Months of standing around draughty church halls listening to dreary political speeches. And hours spent on rainy doorsteps convincing the constituents of Barnes and West

Putney that that nice Mr Major should be given one more chance, all wasted for a quick grope. Not worth it, he thought, but despite his mind's rational assessment of the situation his hand seemed intent on ignoring orders from a higher authority, and it began its four foot journey to its soft objective.

Fortunately for Mackay, Annabel resumed her original position and handed him the piece of paper she had been reaching for into his already outstretched hand. Mackay glanced down at the paper which gave the alphabetical list of streets and developments in the Cresswell Estate. Atlee House, Bevan House, Beveridge Close etc. Even in true blue strongholds like Barnes and West Putney, Mackay had heard that socialists still survived after eighteen years of harassment, bribery, and desertion by the Labour party. Unlike in Kensington and Chelsea (where socialists had been completely eradicated) or in neighbouring Hammersmith and Fulham (where they survived in small dispersed pockets,) his constituency's surviving Reds were all concentrated in one, crumbling, post-war Temple to socialism itself, the Cresswell Estate.

'Why do I get all the best wards Annabel, is it that old Roper doesn't like me?' he said in a mock hurt voice.

'Maybe it's because he sees you as the Party's best salesman Tom,' she replied in her creamy fifteen grand a year Cheltenham Ladies' College accent, 'best equipped for the challenge of Cresswell.' She was too polished to display any sarcasm in her voice or in her expression, but instead of having the desired effect of belittling Mackay it intoxicated him still further.

'It's easy if you truly believe in the Prime Minister and all that we stand for,' he said, folding the piece of paper in an inspired party activist sort of way, 'it's important that we protect what the Government has achieved from left wing wreckers, Marxists and other such destabilisers.'

No response came so he blundered on, desperately trying to think what the Party's current slogan was, 'It's clear to me that if Blair gets over the threshold at Downing Street it will be a disaster, high taxes for all, Britain isn't working.' He suspected that the slogan was not quite right but it rang a bell and his rhetoric seemed to have made an impact on her.

'You're so right Tom,' she said, looking animated. 'I'm sure that the voters can see this. The polls must be wrong. I know we're right. Mrs Thatcher's legacy can't be put at risk. We must win.' She got up from her desk and touched his arm, he felt a slight stirring in his trousers. 'Even enemy bastions like Cresswell Estate can be taken Tom,' she paused, and smiled at him, then continued, 'let's get out there and canvass.'

He looked at her and appreciated her enthusiasm, passion and zeal. For the first time since he had joined the Barnes and West Putney Conservative Party he felt just a little bit fraudulent. She truly had faith in the cause, whereas he didn't give a shit and simply wanted a shag. The tantalising, alluring, pleasing, lingering, thought of the latter, quickly shelved his brief feelings of guilt, and he set off to sample the delights of the Cresswell Estate.

By late afternoon the dozen or so canvassers had returned to Balfour Street for Commander Roper's usual pep talk and debrief. Roper was the archetypal Tory party constituency agent. Always in blazer and tie, with a thick grey moustache (but surprisingly no Victorian sideburns) and the obligatory military bearing and expectation of obedience. He was so stereotypical that Mackay suspected that all was not what it seemed with him. A blemish on his naval record perhaps or some financial impropriety, he wasn't sure which. Mackay noticed Annabel hovering to the right behind Roper and he tried unsuccessfully to catch her eye, but she was too busy feeding the canvass returns into the computer. He desperately hoped that she wouldn't notice the Young's beer stain on the Return sheet for the Cresswell Estate which had been picked up in the Duke of Cumberland about an hour earlier.

'Well people,' began Roper, 'only ten days to go and still a lot of work to do. Our Returns show that it's essential to get our core support out a week on Thursday. Even in a seat like this, there's no room for complacency. What reaction are you getting from the doorsteps? How about the Heston ward Geoff?'

'Wall to wall Blue Mr Roper,' replied Geoff, 'as solid as a rock. Blair can keep his nose out of Heston.' This fighting talk initiated a murmur of agreement from the other canvassers and a stifled yawn from Mackay, who switched off until it was his turn to report. Roper always liked to start with the most winnable wards first, and then carry forward his upbeat message and enthusiasm through to hopeless cases like the Cresswell Estate.

'Any movement in Cresswell Tom?' enquired the Commander after about ten minutes.

'Oh yes. Definitely a swing to us Lawrence,' replied Mackay, (he was one of the few who called the agent by his Christian name). 'Peter Lilley's pension proposals seem to be going down a storm.'

Mackay didn't feel it was an appropriate arena in which to elaborate on the welcome he had received from No. 12 Bevan House. Where, having introduced himself as the representative of the local Conservative Party candidate, the lady of the house had in turn, introduced him to her boyfriend, a man called Headbutt, who in turn had introduced Mackay to his Staffordshire bull terrier, Butch. It was this last introduction which had necessitated Mackay's flight to the Duke of Cumberland and the abandonment of the canvassing for the day.

'I always knew pension reform was a vote winner,' beamed Roper. 'I know we are making an impact. OK, well that about wraps up the debrief, can I count on you all being at the recreation centre in an hour for Question Time?' Mackay joined in the subdued laughter and communal head nodding which followed. Roper's attempt at humorously comparing the gathering of the local parliamentary candidates with the BBC's illustrious current affairs programme, had clearly hit the mark.

The Heath Recreation Centre was just off the Lower Richmond Road. As Mackay entered the 5-a-side football hall he was surprised at the fairly large turn out. There were not only the rosette clad party workers and a sprinkling of local hacks, but also quite a few members of the voting public. The hall was arranged in a similar format to the BBC programme, the only difference being that the 'audience' were not in tiered seating like they were on the real Question Time. The Chairman, complete with Robin Day style thick brown glasses, was the editor of the local Borough Gazette, Roger Metcalfe.

Metcalfe first introduced Paul Smith, the Labour Party candidate, who was, unsurprisingly, the usual local government officer turned trade unionist trouble maker. Then he introduced the Liberal Democrat candidate, who was, naturally, a teacher, though without beard or sandals. Finally there was the Tory candidate, Silas Craven.

Craven was a partner in Mackay's own accountancy firm, Blake and Lander, who after years of trawling up and down the Home Counties in search of a safe Tory seat had eventually fallen on his feet, when he had been proposed by the sitting MP Giles Pertwee, an ex-partner at B&L, who had been forced to stand down after a heart murmur only two months ago.

The debate was light-hearted, even jovial, and ranged over the usual dull topics, the Health Service, Education, Defence, etc. It was only when a member of Joe Public enquired about Tory sleaze that it took off a bit.

Mackay looked more closely at Craven as he defended the Government. He *was* the archetypal City Accountant. He wore a charcoal grey suit with thick chalky white pin stripes, white shirt, light blue Jermyn Street tie and dark blue braces. His hair was largely greying except at the temples, where it was flecked with silver, this gave him the much sought after distinguished look. He was very closely shaven. His eyes were a grey brown colour and impossible to read. His movements were so measured and so smooth that he made the Labour candidate look like a buffoon and the Liberal runner look juvenile. Mackay had to acknowledge that here was a highly polished operator and a brilliant salesman.

'But surely Mr Craven,' continued the determined elderly

lady from the front row, 'you cannot mean that the Government has been completely scandal free.'

'There have of course been one or two lapses by foolish individuals,' replied Craven. 'But the integrity of the Government has remained intact, and as recent polls show, the personal popularity of the Prime Minister remains extremely high.'

At this point, Metcalfe, who was clearly enjoying the role of Grand Inquisitor, half turned to Craven and innocently enquired with a good-humoured smile, 'and what about your own integrity Mr Craven, any skeletons in your past that may come back to haunt you?'

'What do you mean by that remark?' snapped Craven icily.

Mackay, the other candidates, and Mr Joe Public, suddenly became aware that Metcalfe's inoffensive question had released a dose of unpleasantness into the hall. But Roger Metcalfe had missed this, and he ploughed on with his nudge nudge wink wink theme of questioning regardless.

'Come on Silas, we all know what you City accountants are like. Which of us wouldn't let our clients cook their books for the enormous fees you lot get? We know the City's just an Old Boys' network. Don't tell me that you and your firm haven't got your snout in the trough, just like the rest of them.' He had addressed the latter part of his question to the audience, whose anxious faces caused him to turn to look at Craven directly, where he immediately realised that his remarks hadn't been taken in the light-hearted manner in which they were intended. There was a hush in the football hall.

'Do you stand by those remarks?' said Craven, in a legalistic sort of way.

'I was only joking of course,' stammered Metcalfe, rapidly reddening.

'Does that mean you don't stand by those slanderous remarks?' probed Craven.

'No, I mean yes,' replied the Grand Inquisitor, clearly taken aback by the severity of Craven's tone.

Mackay felt sorry for Metcalfe who had simply got carried

away. Craven had unnecessarily humiliated him. The audience sensed this too, as did Craven, who instantly picked up on their sympathy for Metcalfe.

'No harm done then,' he said, his treacly smile rotating from Metcalfe to the audience in a slow 180 degree arc.

Mackay could see that the debate was over and that Metcalfe couldn't get out of the football hall quickly enough. He heard the Grand Inquisitor thank the candidates and audience for coming, announce that the candidates would be available for individual questions for a further half hour, and then after a quick word with a man who Mackay took to be a journalistic colleague, Metcalfe left.

Mackay hung around for a bit, hoping that he could persuade Annabel to adjourn to the Cumberland for a drink. He soon found her locked in conversation with Craven and a voter. This didn't deter him. But as he approached he heard the 'Europe' word mentioned so rather than risk certain tedium he veered off and stood next to Geoff, whom he had earlier seen looking equally as friendless as himself.

Five minutes of Geoff boring him with chat about doorstep canvassing technique was all he could manage, so he suggested that they join Craven who was now talking solely to Annabel.

Mackay felt uncomfortable as he noticed how she hung on Craven's every word and how pissed off she looked when Mackay sidled up to her. 'A polished display Silas,' Mackay said with faked enthusiasm. It was Annabel who answered.

'You handled that awful Chairman brilliantly. Poor man went bright red. You would have thought that a professional journalist ought to know better.' She looked at Craven and he acknowledged her support with a flicker of a smile.

'It's important that we remain focused on the real issues,' said Craven earnestly. 'All journalists are sleaze hunters who don't give a damn about the needs and concerns of ordinary people.'

Craven sounded so genuine that Mackay half believed that he meant it. Geoff certainly did. But more alarmingly so did Annabel. Mackay liked how she had a habit of listening with her mouth slightly open, but with Craven, she seemed to lap up, and almost devour his words in a sexual way. Mackay was glad when Roper joined them but dismayed to discover that Craven had already arranged to drop Roper and Annabel off on the other side of the River on his way back to Knightsbridge. As Roper lived in Fulham and Annabel lived in Notting Hill she would be getting dropped off last, and would be alone in the car with Craven. Craven was married and at least fifteen years older than her.

Craven looked at him as they dispersed to collect their bags and papers and then stepped a foot towards him, entering his personal space. He was so close that Mackay could smell his cologne. He was surprised when Craven then touched his arm in a comradely way.

'Sorry to talk shop Tom,' he began, 'but I have some awful news. Keith Platt was killed in a car accident last night.'

'Bloody hell.'

'A hit and run driver crushed him against a wall as he was on his way home. He died instantly. Did you know him well?'

'Fairly well. A nice bloke. He was going out with Sally Purcell.'

'Was he? I didn't know that. She's in your Department as well isn't she?'

'Yes,' replied Mackay. 'Does she know?'

'Probably not. I'll see it's done. Listen, I know this is very bad timing but Keith was auditing a client of mine, a company called Everyman Credit, it's got a tight reporting deadline and I need a good manager to finish it off ASAP. I noticed from your departmental planner that you're free. Now as you can imagine I'm pretty busy with all this and I need someone I can rely on. Fancy it?'

He looked Mackay directly in the eye. Of course he could compel Mackay to do it but that would necessitate a request to Mackay's departmental partner, which tended to be a political and time consuming procedure. Craven continued to eyeball Mackay and somehow managed to engender a sense of comradeship and loyalty in him, which, despite his endemic cynicism, he found difficult to resist.

'Of course Silas. Anything I can do to help.'
'Great, thanks Tom. If you could pop into my office first thing on Monday I'll run you through it.'
Having got what he wanted, Craven's warmth instantly vanished and it was clear that Mackay had been dismissed. Mackay watched him go, with Roper and Annabel bustling around him, he in a maternal way, she in a possessive way. Mackay decided to have a quick pint in the Cumberland anyway.

As he stood at the bar waiting to order his pint, the man who Metcalfe had spoken to on his way out of the hall and who Mackay assumed to be a journalist appeared at his side.
'Get you a pint?' said the man.
'Ok,' replied Mackay. 'Did you enjoy the debate?'
'Just the usual political crap, though I'll tell you now I won't be voting for your guy. Still want the pint?'
'Of course, are you a friend of Metcalfe?'
'A colleague, I work for him.'
'At the Gazette?'
'Yes.'
'Do you expect me to spill the beans on Craven for a single pint of Youngs?' said Mackay with a wry smile.
'No. I've got a twenty pound note to spend here,' replied the man with a grin.
'That's more like it. Let's sit over there.' The man was about the same age as Mackay or possibly in his mid-thirties. He was wearing a beige sports jacket, open necked shirt and faded blue jeans. He had very short close cropped hair and a worn out look, which was further emphasised by shadowing around his eyes and thick lines at the corners of his mouth and on his forehead. He had a south London accent worthy of the terraces of Plough Lane or Stamford Bridge.
'I don't know much, but what I do know is that there's no scandal for you I'm afraid.' Despite agreeing to do the Everyman audit only a few minutes before, Mackay felt no particular sense of loyalty towards Craven. OK, he was a

partner at his own firm. But Mackay disliked most of the partners at the firm anyway, Craven was no different. He was just a little oilier than the rest of them and somehow more menacing. Was Mackay about to breach any confidences? He didn't think he knew any. If this journalist was prepared to supply him with free drink he was sure he could manage to say nothing slanderous for the two hours that would be needed to knock back six pints.

'Come on there must be something,' said the journalist. 'No string of mistresses, drug taking sons, self-asphyxiation with an orange in the mouth, that sort of thing. What about a nice financial scandal. Did Metcalfe touch a nerve earlier when he alluded to all accountants like Craven being at it?'

Mackay turned and looked severely at the journalist and said savagely, 'what do you mean by that remark?' Unlike Metcalfe half an hour earlier, the journalist held his ground, safe in the knowledge that his remark had been made in a private context, rather than in the public arena of a 5-a-side football hall.

'What I mean,' continued the journalist firmly, 'is that accountants, auditors, call them what you will, I don't know the difference, are all bent. How can they report impartially on a company that pays their audit fees? How can they be objective when they have audited the same company for seventy or eighty years and the partner is a member of the same club as the chief executive? Do they look after shareholders interests or simply their own?'

'Do you stand by those remarks?' said Mackay coldly.

'Yes,' said the man, clearly a little dismayed that he'd misjudged Mackay and that the conversation was rapidly nearing its end.

'Then go and repeat them in front of those people at the bar. You don't know this but Craven is a partner in the same firm I work for, a slur on him, is a slur on me and my colleagues.'

There was a pause as the journalist took a drink from his pint then picked up his wallet and prepared to leave.

Mackay burst out laughing, 'I'm sorry, I'm only kidding.

Get another round in and I'll tell you all about Blake and Lander and Silas Craven, all off the record of course. I'm Tom Mackay.'

'Nick Steadman,' said the man, shaking Mackay's outstretched hand as he got up and headed for the bar.

What a dickhead this guy is, thought Steadman, as he ordered the drinks. Another half hour with him was going to be an ordeal. Metcalfe's instructions to him as he'd departed the Heath Centre had, however, been unambiguous, 'I don't care what it takes. I want dirt on that number-crunching arsehole. I want him nailed.'

Metcalfe had been humiliated by Craven. But both he and Steadman knew that it wasn't usually the place of the Gazette to go digging about the background of Tory prospective parliamentary candidates, such delights belonged to the Tabloids. Still it made a change from the usual cat up a tree type stories which Steadman generally dealt with.

Steadman watched Mackay drain about a third of his pint with his first sup, and then tuck his top lip into his bottom lip to clear away the froth that remained.

'As I said,' began Mackay, 'nothing much to tell about Craven. Been a partner for twenty odd years. Was a fast tracker in his day, just one off the executive board of the firm, but lost out in a power struggle with the current senior partner about three years ago. That ended his rise to the top. Not that he cared much though.'

'Oh, why's that Tom?'

'Well, during the merger frenzy of the accountancy firms in the 80s, which ended with the so called Big 6. Some of the partners at one firm, Blake and Scott, insisted that they get full equity participation in the new firm, Blake and Lander, he was one of them.'

'What does that mean?' pressed Steadman.

'New partners and recently promoted partners will either be salaried or will hold debenture stock in the firm. This means that their payout will be fixed, irrespective of the firm's performance. Craven on the other hand is one of the elite few, who will not only draw out a fixed sum, but who will also share in the pot which is left at the end of the year. In short, he's rich.'

'Why don't the new partners split off by themselves, or at least change the rules to vote one of their own in, as senior partner I mean?'

'Three reasons really. The first is greed. In that occasionally one of them is made an equity partner, and once appointed the newly elected partner very quickly becomes reactionary, rather than revolutionary. The second is that they are very risk averse. Training to be an auditor stamps out any entrepreneurial spirit which may have existed at University. The thought of leaving the comfy confines of a Big 6 firm, with all its legal firepower and status, and going it alone, utterly repels the partners. The only auditors who have balls, are those who set up by themselves and then audit small and medium sized enterprises, that's real risk, but the partners in my firm would see this as grubby. The final reason is the brand. It has taken years and millions of pounds to develop brands like B&L. Irrespective of the quality of the service clients receive, the brand can cover up a multitude of sins and give off a veneer of professional respectability. This hides the fact that the partners are just trying to fleece people, like any other sharp tradesman.'

'You seem bitter Tom,' interrupted Steadman, 'surely Craven's not that bad.' He was keen to steer Mackay back to Craven rather than have him continuing to rant.

'Don't get me wrong. We're not all on the fiddle. But I've seen it happen on several occasions. It's easiest with banks or any complex company for that matter. Including income due in three or even five years time, or using provisions to smooth the bottom line so that earnings show an even year on year increase, anything to keep the analysts happy. Everyone's a winner on the City gravy train. The executives get rich because they meet their targets. The partners get rich on audit fees and lucrative non-core services, such as consultancy. Consultancy is the best wheeze of all. For two million quid, you get a glossy report in which the consultant tells the chief executive it's raining whilst pissing on his head. The only losers are the shareholders, who are far too anonymous to worry about. What's a few pence off the value of their individual holdings, besides,' continued Mackay sarcastically, 'they have the non-executive directors to look after them.'

'I take it you're not intending to make partner then,' said Steadman. 'Won't Craven help you up the ladder? You seemed quite pally with him this evening.'

'No way,' replied Mackay. 'I'm long in my grade already. I'll likely make senior manager in a couple of years then that will be it. I'll probably be farmed out to the HR or the training department. They'll hope that I'll get so bored I'll leave without them having to pay me to go. Craven's had enough of the firm now anyway. He wants to get to Westminster where he can do good and help those less privileged than himself.'

Mackay drained the last mouthful of his pint and tilted the glass from side to side expectantly. Steadman got the message and bought another round. 'What about Craven's family?' he said, after he had pushed Mackay's fresh pint towards him, 'any tearaway sons, tree hugging daughters or bigamous marriages?'

'Nothing there for you,' said Mackay dispassionately. 'No kids as far as I know. His wife Lucilla is an interior designer. I've met her a few times at the office and at the constituency, she's a first rate snob. That's it, apart from he's from up north somewhere. Don't be fooled by the City gent look, he's not Old Money, rather a boy from the Tyne done well.'

'Thanks Tom,' said Steadman. 'Interesting stuff, as you say no scandal but plenty for me to put in my candidate pen portraits in the Gazette.'

They continued talking and drinking, until by closing time, as most boozers do, they had bonded.

CHAPTER 3

(MONDAY 21ST APRIL 1997)

BLAIR SNUBBED AS UNIONS PREPARE SHOPPING LIST
SEAMAN AND SHEARER SET TO RETURN FOR ENGLAND
RAMPRAKASH ADDS STEEL TO NATURAL GIFT FOR BATTING

The advantage of living and working in Zone 2 was that Steadman's commute to work was fairly painless, as his rented flat was only a ten minute walk from work along the Lower Richmond Road. Every morning as he walked, he made a point of looking at the gaps in the housing on the north side of the river through which he could see Putney Bridge tube station, and the barely visible faces of the District Liners standing on the platform.

He imagined them standing there in silence, preparing for the daily scrum which would begin when each tube trundled into the station. He thought back to when he himself had been a District Liner, even then it had been fifty fifty in terms of a seat. Proper platform management could, of course, reduce the odds, but nowadays you had to go out as far as Southfields if you wanted to sit. He remembered fondly that failure to get a seat meant mandatory participation in the post-Fulham Compression, a delightful experience often prolonged by the Earls Court Bottle-Neck. A masterpiece of civil engineering thought Steadman, where forty trains from the Wimbledon, Richmond, and Ealing Broadway lines all tried to get onto the same piece of track at the same time.

Steadman had toyed with the idea of moving out to Southfields, or even East Putney, where the housing was slightly cheaper and where he stood a better chance of persuading a bank to advance him enough to buy a one bedroom flat. In fact, about six months ago he'd even got as far as offering on a flat just by the tube but he'd been gazumped at the last minute. Since then prices had increased a bit, so Steadman had resolved to hang on for a month or two and wait for them to fall again, as they surely would.

The offices of the Borough Gazette were on the top floor of an elongated 60s building which overlooked the river. The building was utterly incongruous with its turn of the century neighbours and Steadman had often wondered how it had got planning permission, even in the 60s. Metcalfe was already in, and he approached Steadman as soon as he'd dumped his Benjy's coffee on his cluttered desk.

'Get anything out of Craven's sidekick on Saturday?' said Metcalfe.

'And good morning to you Roger,' replied Steadman. 'Have a good weekend?'

'Sorry,' said Metcalfe, 'that twat really got under my skin, good morning.'

'The answer to your question is no, not really. The usual dull but lucrative city career, sounds like his wife is quite demanding, no kids, just your ordinary rich bloke ready to move up to the next level of Mazlow's hierarchy of needs.'

'Oh, right,' said Metcalfe with a puzzled look, not wanting to understand, 'that something you learnt in University?'

'Yeah.'

'Nothing else worth looking into.'

'Doubt it. But I'll do the usual trawling about if you want me to?'

'Ok, give it a couple of days.'

Steadman's standard public records sweep revealed that Craven's snobbish wife Lucilla was in fact his second wife. There was nothing unusual in that, but from a journalistic point of view it was interesting because a first wife always tended to have a more newsworthy view of her ex-partner than her successor did. Steadman noted from the marriage certificate that Craven had been married nearly twenty years ago to a Penny Gray, in a place called Alnmouth, which, after a quick consultation of his Collins road atlas, he discovered was a small coastal town north of Newcastle. Then Steadman found Penny Gray's death certificate. There was nothing sinister in this of course, except that a further five hours of digging uncovered an article in a local newspaper, the Northumberland Journal, which, to Steadman's ever increasing curiosity, reported that she'd fallen off a cliff. As he hadn't been out of London proper since before Christmas, he decided to test Metcalfe's resolve to 'want dirt on that number-crunching arsehole.'

He was surprised when Metcalfe approved his northern jolly. Craven had clearly pissed Metcalfe off, as the travel budget of the Gazette barely stretched to Zone 1, never mind the other end of the country. Steadman was sure that Mr Parrot, the proprietor of the Gazette, would not have seen any journalistic merit in his trip, still, he was not complaining, and he booked his ticket on the first train from King's Cross the following day.

As he was leaving the office that evening Metcalfe bounded across to him.

'Where there's a first wife there's always sleaze,' he said. 'Sleaze,' he repeated the word, obviously enjoying mouthing it, especially the long zzzzz part, which he seemed to bite into with his front incisors. 'Sleaze' he said a third time, 'it's endemic in the Tory party, the only known cure is a good long dose of opposition.'

'That's right Roger,' said Steadman, 'the new lot will be no better. OK I admit Blair himself is holier than thou, but what about the rest of them, that Robin Cook, bet he's got a string of mistresses. And what about that big Welsh bloke, what's his name, Davies, Ron Davies, something odd about him, I'm sure of it.'

'Ye of little faith. You just focus on Craven for now, that'll do me.'

'Ok Rog,' said Steadman, putting on his overcoat. 'I'll see you on Thursday. Hold the front page til then.' The joke was an old one often used at the Gazette, a weekly paper, which went out on Thursday.

'Don't bother coming back without at least something,' shouted Metcalfe at the disappearing Steadman, 'and Nick…'

'What?' Steadman's face reappeared at the door at the top of the stairs.

'Don't spend more than two hundred quid.'

'The train fare's one hundred and twenty,' said Steadman incredulously.

'Things are a bit cheaper oop norf lad,' replied Metcalfe, in an embarrassingly bad attempt at a Geordie accent. 'Eighty quid will be enuff to gan you through.' But Steadman was already half way down the stairs as Metcalfe's Gazzaesque tones descended with him.

He liked Metcalfe, who was a reasonable boss and a good teacher. He had rescued Steadman when he'd failed his medical exams and put him on another, more morally, if not financially rewarding career path. Both men knew that Steadman should have left the Gazette and gone to work for a national years ago. When he was motivated, he had the talent and the ability to deliver fantastic copy. But, as had been the case throughout his life, he was stricken with chronic inertia, which, if not remedied soon, would put an end to his dreams of Fleet Street, or more realistically now, Wapping.

In truth, swapping the bright lights of London for some miserable former mining town up north didn't really appeal, but the thought of a night away from his flat and his girlfriend Shannon, did. They had been having problems for a few months now. The major difficulty being that his salary didn't stretch to fancy meals out in the West End or on the Kings Road every night of the week, but, according to her, everyone else's did. Her handbags had to be Louis Vuitton, Versace, Chanel, or at the very least Mulberry. And her unilateral decision that he should pay all of the rent and that she would make up her share, 'in other ways,' had - after the first six months - worn a bit thin, especially when the frequency of the blowjobs had dropped.

Shannon liked everything about London which he had begun to despise. She was in her mid twenties, he in his thirties - in his view, therein lay the problem. Any man who is sick of London is sick of life. Steadman wasn't sure who had said this, probably Samuel Johnson, but he did know that it was bollocks. London was great if you had a lot of money and you could afford to live centrally, if you didn't mind queues and crowds, if you could afford not to use public transport, if you liked grey instead of green, if you preferred fumes to clean air and if you had the energy to battle through it all every day and call it life. Steadman would recommend living in London to anyone, it had to be done, and the T-shirt had to be bought. It was a fantastic experience and had so much to offer for people like Shannon in their twenties, but for Steadman, like most of his contemporaries, five years was enough, ten was far too many, and fifteen years was just plain daft.

At dinner in Enotica that night on Putney High Street, he tried to explain to her where Newcastle was and what he was doing there.

'Isn't it near Scotland?' was her one inquiry.

After which the conversation quickly turned to her work (which was at a call centre just off the A3) and what she planned to do the following night whilst he was away. He was surprised at his own lack of paranoia when she readily confessed that she'd arranged a night out with the girls, which, added to her unusually guarded disclosure as to who the girls were, would normally have aroused his suspicions.

She looked as inviting as ever. Her dark bobbed hair fell repeatedly over her left eye, and she continually arched her back in such a way that her close fitting white T-shirt, which housed her firm pert breasts and large nipples, rode up above her midriff. Seeing that the French waiter had noticed this, and fuelled with most of the wine, Steadman filled up her glass and resolved to shag her as soon as they got back to the flat. Oddly he took a mental note to savour every second of the experience. She had wanted to be more experimental and so this evening they were going to experiment, whether she liked it or not, because he knew that tonight, would be the last time he had her.

The next morning, instead of taking the tube to Edgware Road and picking up the Circle line to complete his journey to King's Cross, Steadman decided to take the overland BR route from Putney to Vauxhall, and then Victoria Line it straight to King's Cross. Unfortunately he discovered that where his platform management skills on the tube might still be passable, he had no idea where to stand at Putney BR. And so despite there being room in some of the forward carriages which whizzed past him, he didn't get on the first train which arrived. The next train, the stopping service, was already twenty minutes late when it eventually came, but it was the very unwelcome points failure at Clapham Junction which really jeopardised his chances of catching the Edinburgh bound 9.05.

This is hell he thought, as he battled down the stairs at Vauxhall with his overnight bag on his shoulder, catching a stationary German tourist full in the face as he accelerated past. Why tourists chose to sightsee through the rush hour, with their enormous rucksacks in one hand, and underground maps in the other, was a mystery. How they had the audacity to ask already distressed commuters the directions to Buckingham Palace or the Tower of London simply beggared belief. Why couldn't they get a cab? There were after all, plenty of cabbies willing to take them to Buck House or the Tower via Croydon, all on the meter of course.

Despite the best efforts of London's transport system to hinder him, Steadman got on the 9.05 with five minutes to spare, and headed north.

CHAPTER 4

(MONDAY 21ST APRIL 1997 - THE SAME DAY)

Irrespective of the time Mackay got up, he took the same train to work every day. If he got up at 6.30, he ended up running to the station to get the 8.50. If he got up at 8.20, he also ran to the station to get the 8.50. It was one of the mysteries and certainties of commuting - you always got the same train.

If it ran on time the 8.50 got Mackay in punctually, but it never did run on time and today was no different. Every day like today, Mackay hid his jacket under his left arm and walked past his boss's office in his shirt sleeves, thus giving the impression that he'd arrived in the office sometime earlier. As he approached, he saw the door was open and he nervously dreaded a summons from within, but thankfully Brendan was on the phone and he skipped past. Across the corridor Mackay could see that Platt's door was shut. He tried the handle but it was locked. He then turned into the already open door of his own office and sat down at his desk.

Mackay had the misfortune to share his office with Tony King. The keenest, neatest, straightest and dullest auditor in a department of boring auditors.

'Morning Tom,' said King. 'Good weekend?'

'Great Tony,' replied Mackay. 'And you?' Mackay didn't wait for the reply. He hung his creased jacket on the back of his chair and headed for the coffee machine. By getting coffee before switching on his computer and spreading a few papers over his desk, Mackay knew that he risked his poor time keeping being discovered, however, he *had* to have coffee, empty desk or not.

A fairly civilised night with that journalist on Saturday had meant that he'd had no hangover on Sunday. On most Sundays the combination of a hangover and work on Monday provided enough of a deterrent to The George. But yesterday being hangoverless, had meant that he'd been unable to refuse Ed's kind offer to buy him a 'quiet one.' That had been at 4 pm yesterday. Twelve hours, one hundred and twenty quid and forty units of alcohol later, Mackay had found himself in the West End's Long Island Iced Tea Bar talking to a divorcee called Brenda. The discussion with Brenda had been vitally important at the time (though Mackay now struggled to remember what it was) and had needed prolonging back at his flat, though once there the conversation had quickly taken on a sexual nature. The full horror of that dialogue, and the awfulness of its conclusion, had only become apparent to Mackay that morning, when he had woken up next to the veteran Brenda, wrinkles and all. Now he stank of booze and the redness of his eyes was nothing short of demonic. He needed coffee.

He returned to his office, grabbed the nearest file and quickly logged on. The coffee was so revolting that it managed to pierce the fuzziness of his brain, and he began to feel more relaxed as he took on the appearance of someone who was working diligently. Did King know about Platt's death? A glance across the room suggested that he didn't. Mackay looked at King again and this time caught his eye.

'Feeling a bit rough today?' said King, in a sanctimonious tone.

'Just a touch of flu I think Tony,' replied Mackay, 'must have got it at that out of bounds thing the other week, hope you don't get it.' He could see that King didn't believe him. Why don't you keep your beak out, thought Mackay? Christ, he hated King, or Wan, as Mackay called him to any sympathetic ear in the Department that would listen. 'You heard about Keith Platt?'

'What about him?' said King quickly.

The phone rang and Mackay picked it up. It was Craven.

'Tom Mackay?'

'Yes.'

'Silas Craven here Tom, can you pop up?'

'Sure.'

'See you shortly then.'

Mackay put the phone down and picked up his pen, paper, and pass.

'What about Keith Platt?' pressed King.

'Killed on Friday in a hit and run on his way home from work.'

'Jesus, where?'

'Victoria somewhere, I'm off to see Silas Craven now to pick up the audit. The audit must go on you know.' King was visibly shocked and Mackay realised that his cynicism had, for once, been misplaced. 'Sorry Tony,' he continued, 'that was a daft thing to say.'

'Hmm,' snorted King.

As Mackay left the room and took the lift to the sixth floor he thought about Platt and King. Whilst he had never got on with either of them, both being as dull as each other, they of course had been kindred spirits and had bonded. Both Company men on the partnership track, both happy in auditland. No wonder King had been so shocked. In his calm measured world of order and stability, death, and especially an early death like Platt's, had no place, it just didn't fit in.

Mackay found Craven's office easily. Unlike Brendan's office, Craven had a room which reflected not only his revered status within the firm, but also his standing as a respected member of the financial community. Mackay entered and saw a picture of Lucilla, Craven's wife, to the right of the large mahogany desk which sat flush under the window at the far side of the room. The desk itself was inlaid with a green leather writing pad around which were placed several neat piles of letters, reports, and booklets, some of which Craven had marked with different coloured post-its. Along the wall to the left was an expensive looking leather settee clearly designed to match the writing pad and also catch the greens in the Constable type rural paintings which adorned three of the four walls. To the right of the room a mahogany bookcase filled with various audit and accountancy books fit snugly between the edge of the desk and Craven's coat stand, where Mackay could see that the beige overcoat and black umbrella were both Burberry. On the far wall, to the left of the window, where anyone entering the room would see it, Mackay noted Craven's framed certificate showing his admittance to the Institute of Chartered Accountants, clearly a source of pride for some he thought. The room had an incredibly comfortable, expensive, reassuring, but above all respectable feel to it, yet Mackay knew that professionally it all stood for nothing, it was simply a veneer.

The partner was sitting with his back to Mackay, the visible part of his red braces forming a cross above the chair like a hazard sign. As Craven didn't seem aware of his presence Mackay cleared his throat. Without acknowledging the signal, Craven continued writing and so Mackay continued to stand.

After about thirty seconds the partner put down his pen and turned slowly in his chair to face the audit manager. Mackay looked away, unable to hold his stare. The warmth and charm of Saturday was gone. Craven looked at him without seeing him, to him Mackay was a nobody.

'Right Tom,' said the partner, 'Everyman Credit.'

'Much to do on it,' said Mackay, trying to sound keen.

'The audit work is finished and I think Keith had just about completed his review. He did mention that there were one or two loose ends which needed tying up. I was due to go out for my review on Friday, I guess we should push that back a week or so now, give you a chance to familiarise yourself with the files and the issues.' He flicked through his standard issue Blake and Lander diary as he spoke, then he continued, 'how's the Department reacting to Keith's death?'

It was obvious that Craven had added the last sentence as an afterthought, and Mackay sensed the partner was internally annoyed with himself, perhaps for forgetting an earlier mental note to ask it first.

'Not many folk know yet,' replied Mackay. 'Any word on catching the driver?'

'No. I spoke to the MD of Everyman about half an hour ago and he said that the police were interviewing staff. Unlikely that any of them were still there that late on a Friday. His name's Jonathan Bridger, nice chap, you'll like him.'

'Anything I should know about Everyman?' said Mackay, 'it's part of Southern and London isn't it?'

'Yes, but only the fag end of the retail lending division. The book started going bad during the recession but Bridger's turned it round. They typically lend five grand to Joe Northerner, who works down pit then loses his job and gets screwed by Everyman on late payment and admin fees. If you add up all the fees their average lending rate is something like fifty percent. They're not popular with the regulator, any excuse and the Bank of England will be down on them like a ton of bricks. No wonder Southern were trying to get shot of them for years.'

Mackay, who was still standing, could see a small passenger jet approaching St Paul's, no doubt heading for City airport. He could hear the engines despite the reinforced terrorist-proof glass in the window. As it flew over the Cathedral it appeared to be speared by the small spire on top of the dome, then it banked left and turned down river. He had been distracted for only a moment but he sensed Craven's irritation.

'Tidy business,' he said quickly, 'they part of what's being flogged to United?'

'Yes, that's the only issue really,' said Craven sharply. 'Because of the takeover we have to make sure the figures are right. Keith thought they were.' He paused then turned back in his chair to face his desk. 'Sorry to be brief, but I've got a meeting at ten. All you need to know is in the file.'

The conversation was over.

Mackay remained motionless, determined to have the last word after his abrupt dismissal. 'What's the address?' he said evenly.

'Sarah's got it,' was the reply.

After a brief pause, Mackay left the room.

Mackay got the address from Sarah, the sixth floor's resident East German shot-putter whose day job was as Craven's secretary. Then he caught a cab to Connaught Lane, which he soon discovered was hidden off Buckingham Palace Road.

Connaught House was a spacious red brick, late Georgian, or early Victorian terraced house with a 1960s extension which ran southwards along the length of the street. As Mackay got out of the cab, he could see that the police had cordoned off the far end of the street and that a large section of the multi-storey car park wall, where Mackay guessed Platt had met his end, was tented off. He signed in with the slovenly looking security guard at the front desk and caught the lift up to the third floor.

There was no receptionist so he went through the dark pine double doors opposite the lift. The room which he entered was the entire third floor set out in open plan, with most of the staff seated in one of two large rectangles. At the far end there were three glass partitioned rooms, the largest of which was clearly the Boardroom. As he walked towards it he was met with several inquisitive stares from bored staffers, a new face providing a welcome break from the tedium.

A middle aged woman who sat outside the smaller office adjacent to the Boardroom spoke to him as he approached the door.

'You from Blake and Lander?'

'Yes.'

'Dreadful business.' She left a decent pause, and then gestured to the Boardroom and said, 'Keith used that room. His files are in that locked cupboard to the right of the flip chart.'

'Where's the key?' asked Mackay politely.

'Keith must've taken it away with him on Friday night,' she said unhelpfully 'you want me to track down the master?'

'Thanks, but give me five minutes first. I'm Tom Mackay by the way.'

'June Paterson,' she replied without looking up from her monitor. 'Jonathan will be in shortly and it's possible the police might want a word with you.'

'Okay,' said Mackay, making his way into the Boardroom. A quick check of the cupboard confirmed it was locked and a cursory scan of the room didn't reveal the whereabouts of the key. He picked up the phone and called Erica, the Departmental Secretary.

'Erica Quirke.'

'Hi, it's me. Can you do us a quick favour?' There was an easy familiarity between them which hadn't been spoilt by a pissed encounter one Friday night a few months back.

'Have you heard Tom?'

'Bout Keith you mean. Yeah, I'm out at his client now, there's police everywhere. Any sign of Sally yet?'

'She's in. No one knows what to say to her. Even Brendan's lost for words.'

'Mmm,...poor lass. Can you find out who the junior was on this Everyman job and get them to give us a ring out here?'

'Will do, Bye.'

'Bye.'

Mackay thought about the distressed Sally Purcell. How Platt had bedded her had been the shock of the year. She *was* the Department Looker with the body to match. Now she was alone, vulnerable, and unattached, though of course for the short term unavailable. Mackay's contemplation of how he could turn her troubled state to his sexual advantage was interrupted by the phone.

It was Kyle Jones. If Mackay was the worst audit manager in the Department then Kyle Jones was the worst junior. They were the two founder members of the Department's Awkward Squad, shop stewards trapped in auditors' bodies.

'What the hell do you want?' said Jones, in his usual respectful manner, 'you looking through my files to see if you can learn something about ticking and bashing.'

'It would help if I could get the pile of shite which masquerades as audit work out of a locked cupboard. No wonder Platt threw himself under a car. I wouldn't fancy reviewing your files.'

'Oh that's nasty,' said Jones with a chuckle, 'try the hollow tube at the top of the flip chart, the black bung thing comes out on the right.' Mackay pulled the phone as far as it would go, and then reached over to the chart. There was no key but the jarring had dislodged something metallic at the far end. He replaced the right hand bung and popped out the left, the key fell into his hand.

'It's on the left hand side you twat. Don't you Welshmen know your left from your right yet?'

'Not my fault dear old Keithy got himself confused.' Kyle paused, 'oh, and Tommy Boy.'

'What?'

'You can keep your filthy hands off the nubile Miss Purcell, what she needs just now is a taste of the valleys and nothing else, Byeeee.' Jones hung up.

Mackay opened the lead file and started to read Jones's near illegible but artistic looking scribble. As he worked his way through the various balance sheet and profit and loss account schedules, he occasionally noticed Platt's neat handwriting giving further explanation as to why the stationary expense was double 1996's or why the cleaning costs had soared during the year, even though only half the building was in use. Mackay yawned, such was the riveting world of audit he thought, still, it warranted enormous fees, enabled him to pay his mortgage and justified Craven's fifty foot yacht.

Whilst reading through the file, what had really surprised Mackay was that Platt hadn't left a 'To Do List.' In all the years they had worked together, first, when Platt had been Mackay's junior, then, following Platt's promotion, when they had been forced to share an office, he'd never known him not to leave a 'To Do List.' Indeed it had been one of Mackay's pet hates. Sometimes, on the rare occasions when Platt had left the office before him, he had sought out the 'To Do List' and added amusing action points at the bottom, such as 'Lick Brendan's arse,' or 'Shag Sally tonight.' Had he been jealous of Platt? Perhaps, but Platt was dead. His life's 'To Do List' irreversibly incomplete.

CHAPTER 5

(TUESDAY 22ND APRIL 1997)

MAJOR OFFERS ALL STATE SCHOOLS FULL CONTROL
IRA BRINGS LONDON TO A STANDSTILL
RUTHLESS HODDLE DROPS JAMES

Despite privatisation, most of the rolling stock at King's Cross was still decked out in BR's old blue and yellow Intercity colours. Steadman's train on the other hand, as befitted the new holder of the East Coast franchise, had dark blue carriages with a thin red stripe running the length of the train and through the gold emblazoned GNER. A fresh coat of paint and a new brand, would that make a difference to Britain's railways thought Steadman. He was hopeful that it would, though for him, the awful almond tasting coffee and forty minute stop outside Stevenage wasn't a good start.

Despite the coffee, the hot carriage and last night's wine soon began to make him feel drowsy. When the middle aged woman diagonally opposite him got off at Peterborough, he was able to stretch out fully and fall asleep.

He drifted in and out of sleep for the next three hours, vaguely conscious of the greater harshness in the accents of his fellow travellers and the greyness of the landscape. At Newcastle, his arrival in the North was confirmed when the train rattled slowly across a bridge over the Tyne. Down river Steadman could see row upon row of red brick terraced housing interspersed with crumbling factories, docks and warehouses. If Britain was booming there was no sign of it here. This place had more in common with Brezhnev's USSR or Ceacescu's

Bucharest than it did with Putney or Barnes. It was no doubt politically closer too. And like Eastern Europe the voters had been powerless for years, eighteen years in fact, but would that change next week? It may do, but he doubted whether it would have any effect here. A second glance out of the window confirmed to Steadman that the place was fucked.

Steadman wasn't looking forward to getting off the train and nosying around. This was not his environment, he didn't feel comfortable and he doubted whether anyone was going to help him. This didn't feel like England to him. He had heard that one of the reasons why the Scots as a race were so cohesive was because a man from Dumfries could readily identify with a man from Inverness, despite living at the other end of the country. He doubted whether many folk on this train had much in common with him, never mind someone from Exeter. This felt like a foreign, hostile country.

About fifteen minutes north of Newcastle the greys started to turn to greens and yellows, the urban hardness giving way to the softer rural landscape. As the train powered on, Steadman began to catch glimpses of the coast. He could see that the North Sea was bordered by very long stretches of golden sand, often curving round wide open bays which frequently ended with a rocky headland topped with a castle or ancient watch tower. Then, after a long right hand bend, Steadman saw what he thought must be Alnmouth. In the distance he could see a row of coloured cottages - with their ochre pantile roofs - in an elevated position above a tiny golden estuary. Stunning he thought, as the train gently braked and began to slow.

As he was the only passenger that got off, the grey whiskered station master, who had waved a green flag to dispatch the express on its way to Scotland, smiled at him warmly and said, 'come far sir?'

'London.'

'Thought so, you look like you need a bit of a holiday.'

'Oh, I'll take it easy then,' said Steadman convivially, 'any chance of getting a cab into town?'

'You'll have to call one from Alnwick, so you're best off

walking, it's only a mile. Go across the footbridge to the southbound platform and walk up the side of the hill from there. Make sure you stay in the Schooner Hotel, it does the best crab soup on the East Coast.'

'Ok I will. Thanks.'

As Steadman crossed the footbridge he observed that the Victorian station had a Railway Children feel to it, complete with hanging baskets filled with geraniums and lobelias, and freshly painted benches. He imagined the grey whiskered station master brush in hand, sprucing up the benches every second Sunday in the month, whilst in order to tend to the hanging baskets, his grey haired wife undertook the more perilous step-ladder work. As he left the shelter of the station and began to walk towards the town, Steadman was glad that the weak April sun decided to make an appearance and attempt to offset the freshness of the sea air.

After ten minutes of walking, the next headland past the town came into view and revealed the ruins of a huge castle about a mile further on. Steadman could see why the medieval builders had built it where they had. The castle was in a great defensive position. Surrounded by sea on three sides the narrow approach from the south was the only land link. He could see that the massive external walls of the main gatehouse were still largely intact as were two towers to the north, but the rest of the outer walls had largely gone.

In a former life the Schooner Hotel had been a coaching inn, and it was through the archway where the coaches had once rattled that Steadman now made his way to the Hotel reception. As the room was empty he rang the brass bell and waited. He glanced casually over the Hotel's promotional literature which lay strewn across the desk, and noted numerous pictures of the castle which he'd just seen. He saw that the fortification was called Dunstanburgh castle, which had been built in the thirteenth century to keep out the Scots. Until then it hadn't occurred to Steadman that where he now stood was in the middle of border country, where only four hundred years ago there had been a real need for thick walls and iron gates.

Steadman rang the bell on the desk again. This time the sound initiated a shuffling noise from the small room behind the desk.

'Can I help you?' said a female voice (with a faint 'please piss off' tone.)

The voice intrigued him, and when she appeared he was not disappointed. She was in her late thirties, smallish, with a splash of long peroxided hair, although the bleach had utterly failed to hide her dark roots. Her face was a bad Jerry Hall/Ulrika Johnson mix, and except for the blue shirt which she wore over her black skirt (instead of the standard white frilly blouse), she was quite definitely out of the Bet Lynch School of Barmaids circa 1979. Indeed, she wore so much makeup that to submerse her would have risked the creation of a small oil slick. Steadman hoped she would be behind the bar that evening and he instantly resolved to make a post-Gordon's pass at her. He knew she was single.

'Have you got a room for the night?' he asked politely.

'Only thirty,' she replied, without a flicker of a smile. 'Just the one night is it?'

'Yeah, what's the rate?'

'Sixty quid - that includes breakfast.' The complete lack of warmth suggested that Steadman's companion was not the proprietor of the Schooner Hotel but rather the hired help. The row upon row of keys lined up in a lockable cupboard behind the desk confirmed that the hotel was empty. But there was no reason why there'd been no attempt to sell him a room with a sea view, which he'd earlier noticed warranted a seventy five pound tariff.

'Any chance of a sea view?'

'You having a romantic holiday on your own then?' she said sarcastically.

'No, I'm working,' Steadman replied nonchalantly. 'I'm a hot shot journalist up from London investigating a national scoop.'

She eyed him more carefully, wondering whether he was being serious, arrogant, or both. 'Do you work for a tabloid then?' He noted the 'please piss off tone' had been replaced with 'now I'm partially interested in you.'

'Sort of. You always lived in Alnmouth?'

'Born and bred. Not much happens round here that I don't hear of. I've worked in this bar far too long and there's not much village gossip that doesn't pass through it. Ask me a question.'

'Well it's a guy called Silas Craven I'm investigating. All I know is that he was married here about twenty years ago, to a woman called Penny Gray. Not much to go on.'

'Never heard of the bloke, but the woman could be something to do with Gray Estates,' she said, warming to the subject. 'There's a big house over by the castle called Branaff Hall. They used to have that but it's owned by the National Trust now. It might be worth you calling in there and getting hold of the guide. It's just opened for the season.'

'Thanks. That's very helpful.' He smiled at her and she smiled back, confirming the sexual attraction. 'You on all day?' he inquired.

'Fraid so. Front of house, the bar, the phone, what's it called…multi-skilled I am.' She turned and reached for a key out of the lockable cupboard and handed it to Steadman. 'Through the door to the right and up the stairs to the second floor, room 207. Breakfast's 7 til 9.30 and the bar serves meals til 9 tonight, unless you want the restaurant that is.' He was disappointed that she hadn't offered to show him the room herself.

'No the bar will be fine,' he said, picking up his suitcase, 'thanks again.'

A National Trust leaflet which he nabbed on his way back through reception about twenty minutes later revealed that Branaff Hall was at the north westerly edge of the village, about half a mile from the Schooner. He set off at once and arrived just as the Hall opened. The building was early Jacobean and still had its original mullioned windows and arched porch, though the fortified square tower at its heart suggested that the present house was built on top of an earlier more defensive structure. The visitor entrance was through the servants' quarters at the back of the hall and - after buying a four pound guide and his ticket - Steadman soon realised that apart from a family of Dutch tourists, he had the house to himself. This enabled him to leisurely quiz the room stewards about anything they might know about the Grays. His guide had given him a brief history, describing how they had been an established Border Reiver family charged with maintaining law and order on this side of the border prior to the Union of the Crowns. The family's fortunes had then ebbed and flowed with the fate of the Stuarts. But decline had become irreversible after the 1745 rebellion and a subsequent lengthy exile, which had seen the management of the Estate neglected. On the present family there was little. The National Trust had taken over the house in the mid 70s in lieu of death duties and there was no clue as to who the living Grays were, or where they now lived.

Despairing that the visit had been a waste of time, Steadman walked towards the more elderly than most female steward in the final room of the tour, the library. She was very old - in her late eighties or early nineties - and he saw that her movements were very slow and deliberate. She sat in the centre of the main library window and seemed to be both looking out to the sea and reading her red leather book at the same time. She appeared not to notice Steadman's approach but a minute, feline like adjustment of her head, indicated that she was aware of his presence.

'Great view,' said Steadman with a smile, 'do you really get paid to look out to sea all day, don't fancy a job swap do you?'

'Yes, I love sitting here,' she said weakly, gradually half turning towards him and looking him full in the face. 'The best views are first thing in the morning when the sun's behind the castle.' Steadman was astonished by the intensity of her gaze and the sharpness of her green eyes. He felt that she was assessing him from head to toe whilst she spoke, and he shifted his weight self-consciously from one leg to the other.

'This would have made a great family home in its day,' said

Steadman cautiously. 'The family were called the Grays weren't they?'

'Yes,' she replied. 'They lived in this house for centuries, and before that in Dunstanburgh itself. They survived the Scots, English Dragoons and even the Revenue, all until about thirty years ago, when they died out after a series of tragedies.' She paused. Steadman felt that she wanted to tell him more - he was certainly keen to find out more about the series of tragedies.

'Oh, what were they?' he inquired innocently. She moved in her chair into what Steadman suspected was her storytelling position, and closed her book.

'Well,' she said, looking at him intently again, ensuring that she had his full attention. 'Basil Gray died without issue in 1975, of a heart attack according to the doctors, but more like a broken heart in my opinion, considering what had gone on a few years earlier.' She hesitated and waited for him to question her.

'What had gone on a few years earlier?' he dutifully asked.

'Well,' she said slowly, rolling the word around her lips, enjoying her control over his keen anticipation. Basil had two children, David and Penelope, both died within two weeks of each other.' She paused, and then stared at him intently so that her hidden meaning was clear. 'Both in tragic circumstances.' She hesitated again, he looked at her luminous green eyes, and then she continued. 'Have you walked the cliff path by the side of the castle?'

'No,' he replied.

'It's treacherous. Very, very treacherous. In fact on a dark windy night when it's raining heavily and there's no moon, whole companies of Dragoons have been known to simply fall off it and go crashing down to their deaths on Greymare Rocks. That's what they say happened to Penelope Gray, fell off the cliff to her death.' Fallings off cliffs and other such tragedies that cut life short were journalists' bread and butter. Steadman felt sure that the readers of the Borough Gazette would be interested.

'And the brother,' asked Steadman. 'What happened to him?'
'Same thing,' replied the old woman, 'but on a tractor.'
'What?'
'If you walk along the path you'll see that the Estate runs down to where the castle's moat was. There's quite a steep hill on the north side and a tractor with defective brakes is likely to go over the edge, which it did - with David Gray on it.'
'Blimey,' said the journalist, 'my readers will love this.'
Steadman had decided to come clean and reveal the purpose of his visit to Branaff. The old woman had been keen to talk, and there was no reason to believe that she wouldn't continue to do so.
'Are you writing a book about the Grays?' she said aggressively. Steadman instantly regretted his decision, fearing that some people simply didn't like talking to journalists.
'No,' he replied defensively. 'I'm a journalist investigating Penelope Gray's husband.'
The old woman threw herself out of the chair at Steadman with such energy that he momentarily thought that she might knock him over.
'Craven,' she said passionately.
As she said this, the family of Dutch tourists entered the room and she looked at them warily. 'Listen,' she said, grabbing his arm and drawing him in closer to her. Steadman dipped his head to listen. 'Let's not talk here, I'm out tonight. But come to Keepers Cottage tomorrow morning at ten, it's the last house in the village just before the start of the castle path. I'll tell you what really happened to the Grays. I'm Anne Gill.'
Clearly exhausted by her exertions she sank backwards and picked up her book signalling that it was time for him to go.
'OK,' he said. 'I'm Nick Steadman. I'll see you tomorrow at ten.' They briefly looked at each other and he smiled at her. She acknowledged it and turned to the window.
Rather than head back to the Schooner straight away Steadman decided to make the most of the fine weather and take the cliff path by the side of the castle. As he walked, he

thought of Anne Gill and how excited she had become at the mention of Craven's name - the half senile ramblings of an old woman or something more?

He soon reached the castle and saw a large hazard sign in the National Trust's distinctive green lettering. The sign warned latter day besiegers of the natural dangers of steep cliffs and slippery rocks, but neglected to mention the man made perils of barbed arrows and boiling oil which ancient attackers had faced. Steadman's assumption that the warning only applied to elderly ramblers was quickly dispelled when the path suddenly narrowed to a few feet, as it squeezed between the wall and the cliff edge. About fifty metres further on, at the point where cliff and wall became one, the path turned a sharp left into the fortress itself and continued through a series of deep internal ditches and trenches until it reached a natural well like hole in the very centre of the castle. Sea spray frothed and boiled up its sides and occasionally spurted out with a force worthy of an Eastern Bloc water cannon.

As he walked further north he was struck again by the stunning beauty of the coastline. In the far distance he could just make out a small island which had at its centre a triangle shaped rock with a castle on top.

'That's Holy Island,' said a gruff voice from behind him. 'That'll be where St Aidan first brought Christianity to these shores.'

Steadman turned and looked at the speaker. The man had a blue peaked cap of the Uncle Albert style and a nautical look to him. He was in his late sixties or early seventies, trim looking but unshaven.

'Really,' said Steadman, with faked enthusiasm, the words 'I thought it was St Columba' dying on his lips. 'Where does the ferry go from? I quite fancy going across.'

'No ferry needed,' said the man. 'You can drive across the causeway from about mid morning til late afternoon at the moment, though I'd check the exact times with the tourist office if I were you.' The man continued to mouth something at Steadman but a huge column of water firing up through the block-hole separated sound from words, so Steadman smiled at the man, nodded his head, and turned back towards Alnmouth.

Steadman returned to the Schooner and rang the bell. There was the expected delay and the standard 'can I help you?' in the same 'please piss off tone' he had heard earlier. Moments later the blonde receptionist appeared from the small ante-room. She smiled at him in a personal rather than commercial way.

'Sorry to bother you again. Any chance I could borrow your phone book?'

She turned to the table behind her, giving Steadman a brief opportunity to study her figure. Where Shannon was thin and slight she was fleshy and ample, in reasonable shape yes, but no one could describe her as lean. Perhaps it was because he fancied trying something different or that he'd simply tired of Shannon's body; either way he found himself irresistibly drawn to her. She sensed this when she spun back round to the desk and caught him gawping at her.

'Here,' she said, handing him the book. He reached out for it, suddenly terrified that he might touch her hand.

'Thanks.'

'Just pop it back on the desk when you've finished with it.' She smiled at him again and he smiled back at her like an awkward adolescent.

There was only one Craven in the book, M.Craven, listed at the Dower House, Berwick Street. Steadman had noticed Berwick Street on his way to Branaff Hall earlier in the day, so having returned the book to reception he set off at once.

The Dower House was an impressive regency building, chunky looking, with large square windows and the distinctive Northumberland arch which Steadman had seen on several houses in the town. He knocked at the door which slowly opened to reveal a small, grey, sprightly looking woman.

'Yes,' she said.

'Mrs Craven,' he said softly.

'Yes,' she repeated with a trace of apprehension.

'My name's Nick Steadman. I'm a journalist from a paper in London covering the election in Wandsworth - where your son's standing.' The last bit was a guess but it soon paid off.
'Yes,' she said for a third time with a slightly relieved look. 'How can I help you?'
'Well I'm just researching a bit on all the candidates - their background, where they come from, that sort of thing. It's important that our readers get to feel that they know the candidates well. After all, it's their votes which will count on Thursday.' She hesitated, clearly torn between her maternal desire to talk about her son and her intuitive wariness of journalists.
'I'd...' She paused, still internally debating, then she continued firmly, her mind made up. 'I'd better check with Silas first if you don't mind. Please come in while I call him. Which paper did you say you were from?'
'The Borough Gazette - by all means call him Mrs Craven.'
Steadman was ushered into a pale green drawing room where he sat down and waited. He heard Mrs Craven speaking to someone on the phone and he suspected that he would soon be leaving. He doubted whether Craven would consent to his interviewing his mother. Indeed it was probable that Craven would react badly when he discovered that there was a journalist sniffing about his home town. He looked around the room and saw several pictures of Craven. Craven as a baby, Craven in school uniform, a youthful looking Craven with a young woman - both dressed in the full 'Shooting Life' uniform. And finally Craven as Steadman had seen him a few days ago, only this time in his Sloane Square gear, and this time with a more sophisticated looking woman on his arm. Steadman hadn't noticed Mrs Craven come back into the room so he was a little startled when she spoke to him from behind.
'I can't get hold of him,' she said. 'His secretary thinks he's somewhere in Fulham.' She walked to the fireplace and sat down in the comfortable looking armchair opposite him. 'What would you like to know?'
'Well just a bit about his early life in Alnmouth - his career,

family life, a pen portrait really. Talking me through those photos might be a good start.'

'Ok,' she said, with no sign of her earlier reservations. 'Let me put the kettle on and I'll tell you all about them.'

Steadman then sat through half an hour of an extremely detailed and very dull account of Craven's childhood. As an only child his mother had been devoted to him, especially after Craven's father had been killed in a mining accident in nearby Ashington Colliery. Steadman was surprised to discover that Craven's father had been a miner, though Mrs Craven was keen to stress on several occasions that although he'd started out as a miner, he'd soon been promoted to foreman. She had tried to be a loving mother, but bringing up a child on a paltry widow's pension had been tough, and it was not until she had secured a position as housekeeper at Branaff Hall that things had got better. Basil Gray immediately took to Silas, developed him over the years, and ultimately got him his articles in Parker & Co, a local accountancy firm. He had then used his connections to get Silas into the City. The road from working class mining family in Ashington to the Conservative Party parliamentary candidate for Barnes and West Putney was a long and unusual one, thought Steadman. And the irony that Mrs Craven now lived in the Estate's Dower House, while the hoi polloi roamed freely over the Hall itself, was not lost on him.

'Who's that?' said Steadman, pointing at the 'Shooting Life' picture of Craven and the young woman.

'Penny Gray,' she said with a sigh. 'Silas's first wife and Basil's daughter, she died tragically on the cliff path, a terrible accident. They were so well suited.'

A touch of the Wuthering Heights about this tale thought Steadman. But it was now clear that he wasn't going to get anything else of value out of Mrs Craven and that his time would be better spent scanning back issues of the local rag in the town library. So he rapidly made his excuses and left.

He returned to his room at the Schooner via the library and a disappointingly empty reception, had a bath, and then went down to the bar for supper.

Steadman examined the bar room more closely. It would have been described as a nautically themed pub in London, with all the standard seafaring kit manufactured on an industrial estate in Slough (circa 1995) hanging on its walls. Except that Steadman knew that because the Schooner had served mariners from Alnmouth's small working port for centuries, the pictures of sailing ships, browning pennants, old fraying ropes and rusted anchors, were all genuine.

Steadman ordered his food and settled into a severe looking wooden booth near to the fire. He began to flick through some back issues of the weekly Northumberland Journal which he had photocopied in the library on his way back from the Dower House. After about ten minutes he found what he was looking for.

7 October 1964 *Northumberland Journal*

LOCAL LANDOWNERS DAUGHTER KILLED IN CLIFF FACE ACCIDENT

Penny Craven, daughter of Basil Gray of Branaff Estates, was killed on Saturday whilst walking the coastal path near Dunstanburgh castle. It is believed Mrs Craven lost her footing in the dark and fell over the cliff whilst walking her dog.

Nothing new there thought Steadman, as he sat eyeing up the incoming tray which the barman was carrying. He was hungry, so the crab soup and lasagne *were* going to taste good, and the bitter *was* going to be thirst quenching.

It was still early and the bar was more or less empty when the shift changed. Steadman was pleased when the barman who had brought him his tray was relieved by the blonde receptionist and he was delighted when she smiled at him shortly afterwards. He gulped down the reminder of his pint and was halfway out of his seat and heading for the bar stool nearest to the pumps, ready to commence his first assault, when the blue peaked cap man of the Uncle Albert style whom he had briefly met at the castle edged in beside him.

'You don't mind if I join you?' he said, almost to himself. 'Enjoy your walk then?' The second question, unlike the first, invited some sort of response from Steadman, so he nodded.

There was a lengthy pause as both men looked at Steadman's empty pint glass. Steadman gave in first.

'Can I get you a drink?' he said.

'Well, only if you're having one anyway,' came the eager reply. 'I'll have a pint of Federation.' Steadman went to the bar to get the drinks.

'Two pints of that please,' he said to the blonde receptionist pointing to the Federation pump, 'and one for yourself.'

'That's very kind,' she purred, and began to pour the pint. 'I see old Joe's latched on to you. Don't worry he's harmless enough. Must say, it's quite unusual for him to pick on a complete stranger like that though.'

'I met him up at the castle, he told me a bit about Holy Island.'

'That explains it, that's just his taster, you'll get the full history now.' She finished pouring the pints and then handed him the frothy glasses.

'Thanks,' he said, looking her directly in the eye. 'I didn't catch your name earlier.'

'Judith.'

'Thanks Judith.' He returned to the booth and put old Joe's pint in front of him.

'Your good health,' the old man said warmly, 'and mine,' he added, the thought no doubt triggered by their difference in age. 'She's single our Judith you know.'

'Really,' replied Steadman, in the most disinterested tone he could manage.

'Never been married,' said the self-appointed matchmaker, clearly encouraged by the neutral response from Steadman.

'That's not to say that she hasn't had her experiences though.'

Steadman looked at him more closely to gauge his meaning and noticed the Sid James twinkle in his eye.

'Quite a few fellas she's been …er…..involved with, all of em bad sorts, time for her to settle down now.'

'I'll bear that in mind,' said Steadman. 'You lived in Alnmouth long?'

'All my life,' said Joe, effortlessly switching from local matchmaker to village sage. The change was detected by Steadman. Here was an opportunity to get the old man's slant on the demise of the Grays.

'I was at the Hall today,' he began cautiously. 'Much as I admire the work of the Trust. I always think it's a shame to see these old houses turned from homes into museums. Pretty tragic end to the family that lived there I was hearing.'

Joe's eyes lit up. He glanced quickly from side to side in much the same way as René would have done had the Schooner been instantly transported to Vichy France. Steadman heard the bar door open behind him and he turned to look, half expecting Herr Flick to walk in, but instead it was the Dutch tourists he'd seen at the Hall earlier in the day.

'No tragedy about it,' said the old man drawing closer to Steadman. 'A family curse - started in the early seventeenth century by Edmund Gray, Warden of the English East March.'

'Warden of the English East March,' repeated Steadman. 'What's that?'

'Well,' said Joe, relishing the question. 'Before the Union of the Crowns in 1603 the area round here was border country - a long way from London and the authority of the English Queen, and a long way from Edinburgh and the Scottish King. A lot of thieving went on at full moon, especially of cattle, this was known as 'Riding' or 'Reiving.' The closer to the border you were the more lawless and barbaric it got. All the inhabitants belonged to a family or clan and they stuck together, aiding fellow clan members if they got into trouble, ancient blood feuds were commonplace. In order to keep some sort of law and order, both monarchs appointed three wardens and the border territory was divided into East, Middle, and West Marches. Of course offences committed in their own Marches could be dealt with by their own courts. But the wardens on both sides of the border had difficulty in dealing with criminals from the opposite March - who often stole cattle then fled to the other side of the border.'

Joe paused briefly for breath, and then continued. 'To deal with the problem Wardens agreed to meet their opposite numbers on 'Days of Truce' - where those attending had safe conduct from sunrise to sunset in the appointed town. Having given assurances to each other about the truce, they would then form a jury of six Scottish gentlemen appointed by the Scottish Warden and six English gentlemen appointed by the English Warden. This jury tried the Reivers. The 'Days of Truce' became a sort of bank holiday fair - where hawkers and tinkers would set up their stalls and all would have a gay time, except of course the convicted Reivers, who were hanged.'

'What's all this to do with the Grays?' asked Steadman.

'Well, the problem with the system was that the March Lords were often drawn from the border families, so impartiality and the objective dispensing of justice could prove difficult. The Wardens were usually the biggest crooks of all. Their office seen as a way of enriching themselves and their families - a gift for services rendered to the Queen, which in the case of the Grays was unusual, because they were Catholics. For a long time the patronage of the Queen ensured their protection from their ancient blood enemies - the Taits, and in particular Willie Tait, Warden of the Scottish East March.'

Old Joe finished his pint and Steadman was dispatched to the bar for refills. He saw that it was dark outside now and that the bar was more or less full. The patrons no doubt drawn to the enormous blazing log fire which threw its light out onto the road in sharp red and orange tongues. He was eager to hear the next instalment of Joe's story, so Judith was smiled at rather than spoken to whilst she pulled the next round. He returned to the booth. 'We'd got as far as the Taits,' he said.

'Well, it was late March 1603 when the 'Day of Truce' was

called and it was agreed that it would be held in the small market town of Calder. Now Edmund Gray was determined to get even with Willie Tait, seeing as he'd hanged one of his own cousins as a Reiver the year before. It was fortunate for Gray that as he journeyed to Calder he met Sir Robert Carey, who was on his way to Edinburgh to fetch King James down to London as Queen Elizabeth's successor. Fearing an end to the system and his own position, Edmund decided to act. The next day Willie Tait and his retainers arrived in Calder assuming that they would be guaranteed safe passage - but unaware of the Queen's death, they were all taken completely by surprise and hanged on trumped up charges of treason.'

'But weren't the Grays punished by King James?' said Steadman.

'No. The King was unsure of his own position at the beginning of his reign. And by the time he'd fully established himself he'd become so anglicised that he'd forgotten all about his Scottish nobles. He never returned to Scotland once you know. But as Willie Tait stood there on the gallows waiting for the drop, he looked at Edmund and cursed him and his family. 'The Grays shall never grow grey,' he shouted at the crowd. And that's how it's been. No male members of the family have ever reached fifty. Cursed they've been from that day to this - and now they're all gone. Basil Gray was the last. Died of a broken heart about twenty years ago after his son and daughter perished on Greymare rocks, just below where I met you today. Tragedy some say, cursed I say.'

Steadman nodded. The yarn was over. They continued to talk about Alnmouth life in general and how it compared to London living, about Joe's time on the boats and about journalism. It became clear that there was nothing new on Craven and Steadman noticed that it was only an hour before closing time. He saw that the stool he'd set off towards earlier was still free, so a late sortie to the bar was still on. With Joe's blessing he moved to the bar and sat himself down on the stool. His intent was clear and Judith read the signals. As none of the customers was close to ordering a drink she picked up the large gin and tonic she'd hidden behind the till and came round to the customers' side of the bar and sat down beside him.

'You come here often?' he said humorously with a Roger Moore raised eyebrow and a silly smile. She laughed. And when the bar had emptied they were still talking.

CHAPTER 6

(WEDNESDAY 23RD APRIL 1997)

MAJOR INSISTS TORIES CAN STILL WIN
POLL SHOWS LABOUR 15 POINTS CLEAR
HESELTINE CALLS POLLSTERS CLOWNS

Mackay had a phone next to his bed. If it hadn't been by his bed when it rang at 7.30 that morning it would have gone unanswered. The voice on the other end of the line was clearly a native English speaker but the accent was strange, and Mackay was unable to place it.

'Thomas Mackay,' said the voice.

'Yes.'

'Thomas Mackay of 17D Garlieston Street, Putney, London.'

'Yes. Can I help you?' said Mackay quickly, and in a tone which suggested that he was beginning to wonder whether the caller was some sort of foreign law enforcement officer, Interpol perhaps.

'Mr Mackay, my name is John Benady. I'm a partner in the firm of Likudi, Benady, Gomez and Scott solicitors, here in Gibraltar. I do apologize for calling at such an early hour, however, I wanted to try and catch you before you went off to work as I don't have your work number.' Mackay was intrigued. What did they want with him? He had never been to Gibraltar before.

'Mr Mackay I'm afraid I have some very bad news. Your uncle, Joe Sharp, sadly passed away yesterday.' Benady paused to let the news sink in and then waited for the usual sign of surprise, shock, or early grief. As there was only silence, he continued with the same quality of measured calmness in his voice. 'The reason for my call Mr Mackay is that your Uncle's will - which I have here in front of me - appoints you and me as joint executors of his estate.'

'Where and what did he die of?' asked Mackay.

'A heart attack at his villa in Jimenez,' replied Benady. 'By the time the ambulance arrived I gather that he'd already been dead for some time. It's unlikely that he suffered.'

'That's the best we could hope for. What do we do now?'

'Well the first thing is to get probate, and then we can access his funds and begin discharging his liabilities. It's likely that getting to that stage will take a month or two. After that we can start distributing the estate to his beneficiaries.'

'Am I a beneficiary?' asked Mackay, a little too hurriedly.

'Yes. You, your sister and your cousins get equal shares,' replied the solicitor.

'And the size of the estate?'

'Difficult to put a precise figure on it. There's the villa in Jimenez, some property in the UK, shares, and quite a lot of cash. Fortunately it was our firm that helped your Uncle a few years ago when he ran into difficulty with the Inland Revenue.'

'More than a million then,' pressed Mackay.

'Forgive me. But it's not easy to be certain,' squirmed the lawyer. 'Property values, the shifting equity markets…'

Mackay interrupted and did his best to sound authoritative. 'Go on. What's your best guess?'

'I think a million pounds is as good an estimate as any at this stage,' replied the solicitor evenly. He paused, giving Mackay time to mix the genealogy with the arithmetic. 'The thing is Mr Mackay, I really need your signature on a number of documents to get things moving as soon as possible. Plus it would be useful to have a thorough discussion with you about our strategy in terms of asset disposals. Your Uncle had a couple of investments for example, which even at this early stage, I would strongly recommend remain...' He hesitated. Then continued in a soft conspiratorial manner, '…shall we say

...off-shore.'

There was a further pause as both men took stock of the conversation. Benady wondering whether he'd gone too far, and Mackay wondering whether 'off-shore' might present opportunities for him which would be denied to his cousins.

It was Benady who spoke first. 'If you could spare the time Mr Mackay, it might be worth you coming out to Gibraltar. It'll probably be more efficient spending half a day in the office here and signing all the papers at one sitting rather than me sending over reams of documents in drips and drabs and you sending them back. What do you think?'

Mackay knew that Ryanair and Easyjet were expanding rapidly, but he was pretty sure that the Gibraltar route still remained the preserve of BA. As a rule - unless the client was paying - lowly audit managers never paid for BA flights out of their own pockets, so the thought of paying his own way to get to Benady's office did not immediately appeal.

Correctly sensing that Mackay's hesitation signalled his reluctance, Benady continued. 'Of course your expenses would be met from the estate. Shall I see if I can book you into the Rock Hotel? It's starting to get busy at this time of year but I know the manager very well. In fact, why don't I see you in the office first thing on Monday morning? You and your wife could fly out on Friday and make a weekend of it.'

Of course there really was no comparison between the prospect of sunning himself in warm Mediterranean climbs and another weekend spent trailing hopelessly around the Cresswell Estate - being berated by the likes of Headbutt and hounded by Butch. So Mackay readily consented and agreed to meet Benady at 9am on Monday morning at Linewall Road, Gibraltar.

As it wasn't yet 8.00, Mackay was tempted to have another twenty minutes in bed, but then he remembered he was a professional and got up. He was in Victoria and at his desk within the hour, strangely motivated, though this soon started to leak away after an hour spent with the audit files. The absence of Platt's 'To Do List' continued to irritate him, not only because it was unusual, but also because it meant that he'd to do a full re-review of the files himself, rather than just look at the outstanding bits which Platt had left.

The morning passed quickly and after a liquidish lunch in the Duke of Connaught, Mackay decided to review the income section of the files. He soon saw some notes in pencil which Platt had made in the margins of one of the schedules. The writing had been rubbed out but Mackay could still make out the words, 'Insurance rebate £7m,' which his predecessor had also underlined. This was odd because there was no 'Insurance rebate' caption shown in any of the lead or supporting schedules, nor could he find any trace of it in any of the account balances which had been spewed out by the computer. What sort of insurance did Everyman have? There was the usual buildings' insurance, and employees' and directors' liability insurance, but these amounts were small and would not have been material enough to warrant further investigation by Platt. Mackay decided to ask the MD what this rebate was at the first opportunity, which occurred mid-afternoon when Jonathan Bridger called him into his office.

'Please, come in Tom.'

Bridger used the open palm of his hand to invite Mackay to take the seat opposite his desk and sat down himself. He smiled at Mackay warmly and the auditor looked at his client more closely. He was in his fifties yet he still had a full head of tawny brown hair which he combed to the side of his head with a touch of Brylcream. He was well over 6 ft, probably nearer 6 ft 3, and in good shape with just a hint of a banker's paunch. His face was hard lined, almost geometric. His plain dark blue suit was Jermyn Street, as was his plain pink shirt, but his blue tie had a small motif or shield in the centre of it, which Platt took to represent membership of some exclusive Edinburgh Club, maybe the New Club.

'How's it going?' asked Bridger.

'Very well thanks. Most of the work's been done already. Keith did a good job.'

'Yes. I thought he would, struck me as a very thorough guy, a terrible shame.'

'Yes,' replied Mackay, 'it was.'

There was a long embarrassed silence. Bridger spoke first.

'Is everyone being as helpful as they can? Just let me know if there's anything I can do.'

Mackay, like most of his profession, didn't like running across awkward audit issues. His usual solution was to book himself on the following year's audit as soon as possible, then leave the problem alone, hoping that it would disappear by the time he revisited the books twelve months later. He surprised himself when he asked the following question. 'Well Jonathan, there is one thing that's troubling me…'

'Oh, what's that?' replied the banker, sitting slightly back in his chair and clasping his hands together.

'Keith left some notes indicating that Everyman was due an insurance rebate of some kind. Do you know anything about it?'

'No, I don't,' said Bridger. 'Colin might know something, but he's not well at the moment.' Colin Brown was Everyman's Financial Controller.

'When do you expect him back from sick leave?'

'Difficult to tell with stress, not soon though.'

'Does anybody else know anything about it?'

'Unlikely, Colin's your man. I'll send an email around the Accounts Department. We may get lucky.'

The auditor and client looked at each other carefully. Mackay felt uncomfortable. Bridger's reply had been a bit too prepared and measured. Surely a more natural reaction would have been one of concern, or at least of further inquiry. On the other hand perhaps he was being paranoid, and Brown did have an explanation for it after all.

'If there's anything else you need, don't hesitate to ask,' said Bridger, with a salesman's smile.

Mackay got up to leave and headed for the door. After a couple of steps he half turned to face Bridger, who had clearly been watching his exit, 'Oh, just in case you're wondering where I am on Monday, I'm having the day off.'

'Going somewhere nice for the weekend?'

'Gibraltar, to sort out my uncle's estate, he died yesterday.'

'I'm sorry to hear that, were you close?'

'Not really. I haven't seen as much of him since he moved out to Spain, he was great fun when I was a kid though.'

'Well I know it's not a good time, but try and make the most of the Rock. It's the best place the Bank ever sent me, and the views from the summit on a fine day are the best in Europe.'

'OK, I will.' He looked at Bridger, who was staring blankly at him, still in the midst of nostalgasising about the happier days of his youth. And for some reason he felt sorry for him. Mackay returned to the Boardroom and hurriedly packed up. Uniquely for him, and in accordance with standard audit practice, he locked the files away properly and took the key with him.

It was late in the afternoon, but instead of calling it a day he decided to return to Blake and Lander's offices. He picked up an early edition of the Standard and caught the next eastbound District Line train. As the tube idled outside St James's Park, he glanced casually at the first few pages. The latest polls made grim reading. This election is a joke thought Mackay. His absence from the Cresswell Estate frontline this weekend was going to make bugger all difference. Major was already yesterday's Prime Minister.

As the tube left St James's Park, Mackay was surprised that no one came to claim the large suitcase which rested on the other side of the partition from him. He looked around the carriage. Seated facing him was an Indian woman dressed from head to foot in black, and to his right, were three shabbily dressed businessmen all in creased grey suits. A middle-aged, badly dyed auburn hair woman in a bright green coat stood on his side of the carriage at the next door.

Mackay's decision to reclassify the suitcase from attended to unattended was driven principally by the fact that when it went off he would have the full benefit of the blast all to himself. Christ, he was being paranoid now, but the suitcase did bother him. It had nearly toppled over after the last left hand bend and any further lurches to the left might prove fatal. He looked again around the carriage, but none of his fellow travellers had any interest in the suitcase whatsoever, in fact, the only response he got was a hostile glare from the Indian woman who no doubt thought that he was ogling her. He looked more closely at her and noted that she did indeed have an attractive Bollywood type quality to her. The carriage lurched to the left and the suitcase tipped thirty to forty degrees off its base, then settled back against the partition. Mackay could feel his heart beating quickly and a cold sweaty film developing along his spine. There was nothing for it but to act.

'Is this anyone's suitcase?' he asked, addressing the carriage in his best Scotland Yard voice.

There was the usual, 'God, I hope you're not speaking to me,' delay, which Londoners adopted when anyone spoke on public transport, but the implication of Mackay's question did provoke a reaction from the three businessmen, who began to eye the suitcase nervously.

One of them shifted his gaze to Mackay and said, 'nothing to do with us mate.'

'It's mine,' came a very welcome Antipodean cry from the door. It was the middle-aged badly dyed auburn hair woman with the bright green coat, who then walked along the aisle and casually took possession of the suitcase cum suspected semtex carrier. She smiled at Mackay as the train pulled into Westminster, picked up the suitcase and proceeded to get off. Having disembarked, she turned to Mackay and said with a cheeky look on her face, 'I'm off to blow them up.'

'Make sure you get all of them,' replied Mackay. The door closed and the tube set off towards Embankment.

Mackay got to the office without further incident and was glad to discover that he'd the room to himself - Tony King being out at a client. The insurance rebate still bothered him. If it was a rebate then there had to have been previous payments at some stage, and these must have been recorded. As it was before 5.30 he rang up the post room and commissioned a priority recall of the previous years' audit files. As the archived files were held offsite, he was told that it would take an hour to get them, so he decided to use the time constructively in the Bell Inn on Fleet Street.

He put on his jacket and was about to leave when Sally Purcell stepped into his office.

'You OK?' he said, as sympathetically as he could manage.

'Fine Tom, you off somewhere?'

'I'm going down to the Bell for an hour or so, fancy a drink and a chat?'

'Only if it's a double, come on.'

They found a secluded table in the bay of the pub's frosted window. She had a double gin and tonic, and he, due to the lack of Young's, had a London Pride.

'You're doing Keith's audit,' she said, as a neutral opener.

'Yes, not much to do on it, you know what he was like, pretty thorough.'

'Yes,' she replied.

Would she burst into tears at the mention of his name? He doubted it. She and Mackay had been close once and he'd got off with her during the two week induction which the firm put on for all new graduate trainees. There had been sexual chemistry there then, but that had been it. They had remained kindred spirits, and shared a common bond of cynicism, but Mackay had always been disappointed that their relationship had developed in a platonic way. He could not understand what she had seen in Platt.

'Listen Tom, I'm glad I caught you in the office. I need someone who understands me to talk to, my relationship with Keith was on its last legs and I'm sick of being the recipient of so much unwarranted sympathy. I was bored of him and I was going to dump him last Friday, there, I've said it.'

Having got so much angst off her chest, which Mackay had seen was looking even more substantial than usual, she finished her drink in a single gulp and got up from the table.

'My round then,' she paused, and looked at him, 'same again?'

He was caught a bit off balance by her unexpected revelation but he still managed to splutter out, 'No, I'll try a Shepherd Neame Spitfire this time.' She turned and headed for the bar. He took a large swig out of his glass whilst he waited for her to return. Mackay looked at her as she stood at the bar. She was petite, curvaceous, and very, very, very, attractive. Her hair was discreetly highlighted and loosely bobbed almost in a boyish way. He had always found her mouth irresistible, but her most eye-catching feature was her large blue eyes which simply drew Mackay in.

She returned with the drinks and he put the empty glasses from the previous round onto the next table. They continued to talk and drink. They gossiped about people in the Department, about the election and Mackay's escapades on the Cresswell Estate (at which she laughed), and about his unsuccessful pursuit of Annabel and of his worry about Craven's predatory behaviour towards her.

'Craven's an oily one,' said Sally. 'He was leching after me at a Christmas Party a couple of years ago. I can see why some women go for him though.'

'Why's that Sal?'

'He kind of envelops you with quality. Quality clothes, smells, gifts, cars, he makes you feel you'd be safe with him and well looked after. He gives you all the things you always wanted from your father, plus, he has the maturity a girl always wants from a partner. He looks good and I bet he'd make a great lover.'

'Sounds like you've thought of him before in this light Sal,' said Mackay teasingly. 'You sure nothing came of that Christmas Party?'

'What and then I fled into the arms of reliable dull old Keith when it all ended in tears?'

'Yeah, something like that.' Her remark had been light-hearted but Mackay couldn't help wondering whether there might be some truth in it. True or not, he didn't really care, just as long as she next fled into the arms of unreliable stimulating old Mackay.

'Listen Sal, I know you won't believe this, but I've got to get back up to the office. I've recalled some files from archives which I fancy having a quick flick through before I head off.'

'Most unlike you Tom,' she said. 'What's so important?'

'Oh nothing, just a loose end from Keith's audit.'

'Well why don't we have another drink then I'll come up with you and we can go through them together.'

'Great,' he replied, surprised by her offer of help. 'But why the sudden desire to join the evening audit shift?'

She got up and headed towards the bar. 'Don't worry,' she said with her back to him, 'you'll be paying for dinner.'

He quickly finished his pint. Where the hell was this evening leading to?

Until their liability is limited by the seven year period set by the Companies' Act, all audit firms kept files covering their previous audits. Those files evidenced Blake and Lander's most important product, audit opinions. In theory the files were all that stood between angry creditors and the partners' homes in Guildford if things ever went wrong. Things never did seem to go wrong though, and if they did, firms always settled rather than go to court, thereby avoiding any dangerous precedents which could be referred to later. As Blake and Lander had won the Everyman audit in 1991 there were upwards of thirty files contained in the four large boxes which now sat on Mackay's desk.

'What are we looking for Tom?' asked Sally. He told her about Platt's underlined notes indicating a possible seven million pound insurance rebate of which there was now no trace.

'I'm sure there's a reasonable explanation for it Sal, we'll no doubt find the answer in these boxes.' He paused. 'That's odd.'

'What?'

'Look, someone's had these boxes out recently.' Underneath the gold 'B&L' which was emblazoned on each box, there was a red grid which the archivists used to track where each box had been. In the 'out' column on all four boxes there was the date 15 April '97. And in the 'In' column was the date 22 April '97.

'Unusual that Keith got out all the previous year's audit files,' continued Mackay, 'he must have been looking for this insurance thing as well.' He took out his keys and began cutting through the brown tape which sealed each box, then he suddenly stopped again, 'that's even more puzzling Sal.'

'What is, Tom?'

'These boxes were sent back to the archives a week after they were got out, on the 22 April, yesterday.'

'So what of it?' she replied.

'Question is, who sent them back Sal? Keith had been dead for five days.'

'Mmm…I suppose he could have emailed instructions to Erica or one of the other girls,' she said unconvincingly.

'Possible, I'll check tomorrow.' Of course it was possible but it wasn't likely, no one was that anal, not even Platt. Mackay began to feel uncomfortable about Everyman, was there something weird going on or was it just an odd set of circumstances?

'Nothing in this box,' said Sally, 'they're mostly balance sheet files.'

Mackay continued to look through his two boxes also without success. 1995, 1994, 1993, each file looked remarkably similar to the previous year's, and reminded Mackay of the age old audit joke, 'why did the auditor cross the road, answer, because he did it last year.' Every year profits were ten percent up on the year before, and every year there was a corresponding year end adjustment in the company's provisions, just to make sure that the profit growth was nice and smooth. Mackay chuckled to himself as he flicked through the 1994 file - he saw that Everyman had had a bumper year and recorded profit before provisions of £14.4m, a twenty percent jump on the 1993 figure. The same year a £1.2m provision for redundancies had been booked, so the final profit figure which had been submitted to the Group had shown only a ten percent increase year on year. He picked up the 1995 file again, a poorer year, and saw that the profit before provisions had dropped to £12.5m. But this had been okay because Jonathan Bridger had obviously felt that redundancies were not necessary after all, so the £1.2m provision which had been made the previous year along with a further £1m from a few specific provisions had been released to profit. All this meant that the final figures which were released to the Group showed a ten percent increase in profits year on year.

'Sal, I bet Bridger's bonus is contingent on Everyman hitting ten percent a year profit growth, some of these provisions are a joke.'

'You've seen who the partner's been since 1991?' she replied.

'What, Craven?' he said incredulously. 'On the same job for six years, you're kidding, you really can't beat a bit of auditor independence - now what's this?' He had been flicking through the 1991 file and saw that in the general correspondence section there was a letter from the Avon and General Insurance Company, which read as follows;

Avon and General Insurance
23-27 Bernard Street
Bristol
BS8 6NE
Tel. 0117 909 6000
Fax. 0117 909 6001

Jonathan Bridger
Managing Director
Everyman Credit Limited
No 2 Connaught Lane
Victoria
LONDON
SW1 7RQ

17 June 1991

Dear Jonathan

Master Credit Insurance - Policy No. CF/89/762

Further to our telephone conversation yesterday, I confirm that due to the low number of claims submitted under the terms of this policy, no further premiums are due.

Yours sincerely

Angus Cook

ANGUS COOK
Senior Underwriter

Mackay then turned to the payments section of the file but discovered that the key schedule which dealt with the insurance costs was missing.

'Look at this Sal,' he said excitedly, 'could be what we're looking for.' He showed her the letter and the missing costs page. 'Funny how there's no mention of Avon and General in any of the other files we've been through, almost as if someone's been through them.'

'You see conspiracies everywhere,' she said flatly. 'I'm sure there's a perfectly sensible explanation.'

'Sal, I asked him directly about this and he denied any knowledge of it.'

'Could be any number of reasons,' she said firmly, clearly determined to deflate his excitement. 'Let's call it a day and grab something to eat. I'm off to powder my nose and pack up my desk, and I want you ready to go in ten minutes.' As she said this she lightly touched his arm and moved towards him just enough to enter his personal space.

'Ok,' he said a little sheepishly. A suggestion, request, instruction, command or decree, it made no difference if the words came from Sally Purcell's lips. There was an expectation that men would obey her and wish to please her, Mackay was no different.

She left the room and he quickly walked over to the other side of his desk and picked up the phone. The number he called for Avon and General Insurance had changed. But with the help of the operator he got the new telephone and fax numbers, and was soon able to confirm that the Company was still at the same address as it had been six years ago. Then he sat down at his desk and typed the following letter;

Blake & Lander
No.1 Sir Thomas More Square
Temple
London
EC6 7EB
Tel. 0171 552 8909
Fax. 0171 552 8910

Contact: Tom Mackay

Avon and General Insurance
23-27 Bernard Street
Bristol
BS8 6NE

23 April 1997

Dear Sirs

Everyman Credit Limited
Master Credit Insurance - Policy No. CF/89/762

As part of our audit procedures and in accordance with the instructions of our mutual client, Everyman Credit Limited, we would be grateful if you would fax to us, at your earliest possible convenience, copies of all the correspondence between yourselves and our mutual client since 1 January 1992.

Yours faithfully

Tom Mackay

TOM MACKAY
For Blake & Lander

Jonathan Bridger

JONATHAN BRIDGER
For Everyman Credit Limited

Well, thought Mackay, if the beauty of modern technology (the use of electronic signatures) meant that he could tailor a standard audit bank letter and use the amended version to obtain unauthorised documents then all was well and good. Surely it was a legitimate part of the audit anyway, and clearly the end justified the means, did it not? If he faxed this letter, was he committing a criminal offence? He didn't think so. He certainly didn't have Bridger's or Craven's authority to ask Avon and General for these documents, and it was probable that his proposed actions were likely to get him into trouble. In fact, what the hell was he doing? Had he forgotten that he didn't give a shit? He could hear Sally come out of her room and head for the Ladies, it would be time to leave the office shortly, so he faxed the letter.

CHAPTER 7

(THURSDAY 24TH APRIL 1997)

KNIVES OUT FOR MAWHINNEY
IS HODDLE BEING DEVIOUS OR JUST PLAIN DAFT
FRASER SHOULD WIN VOTE OVER SPIN DOCTORS

Mackay got up the next day and felt seedy rather than hung over. Despite plying Sally with several more gins and a half bottle of Jacobs Creek during supper, he had got nowhere near enticing her back to his flat. But surprisingly she had agreed to go to Gibraltar, expenses paid of course, and share a room with him on a purely 'no sex basis.' In the cold light of day, would she still come, and if so, would the warm Mediterranean sun work to his advantage?

Instead of getting off the tube at Victoria, Mackay decided to go to Temple to see if there had been a response from Avon and General. Predictably Tony King was already in the office and moaning about the boxes stacked on his desk. Mackay noticed that he looked even duller than usual. 'Sorry, I'll get one of the juniors to move them.'

'You know that files are supposed to be in locked cabinets overnight, even in the office,' said King.

'Well it was pretty late,' replied Mackay defensively, with a huge evidential yawn. Christ, just talking to King made him feel tired. King was like a bespectacled parasite, drawing energy from his hosts, then chewing it up and spitting it out in large dollops of audit waste.

Their shared fax was empty, and as there was nothing in his

pigeon hole except a technical brief about FRS 7 (Fair values in acquisition accounting) which went straight in the bin, Mackay left the room and headed for the juniors' area. Kyle Jones wasn't there, so he called into the secretaries' room where he found the Welshman flirting with Erica Quirke.

'I'm glad I've caught you both,' began Mackay, 'have either of you moved or sent any of Keith's boxes back to archives in the last few days from that Everyman audit he was doing?' They both shook their heads.

'Could have been Julie though,' said Erica, 'she sent something down the other day, but she's off sick again. I had a look for the departmental archive records yesterday but I couldn't find them. Jules must have put them somewhere.'

'Can we call her?' asked Mackay, a little frustrated that the system should collapse because of the absence of the junior secretary.

Erica looked panicked. 'I've tried her on her landline and mobile already, she must have been asleep.' Mackay sensed that Julie's sick day might have been integral to a long weekend spent somewhere nice, and that Erica had been asked to cover for her. Having done the same himself on a number of occasions, he didn't press any further.

'Well if you *do* manage to get hold of her, put her through to me at Everyman,' he said with a knowing smile. Erica got the message and looked relieved. 'Kyle, did Keith ever mention a large insurance rebate to you when you were out there with him?'

'No boss,' he said sarcastically, 'we only crossed over for half a day, said he would prefer to do a cold review rather than have me hanging around, made no mention of an insurance rebate.'

'You're sure he always left the key to the audit cupboard on the right of the flipchart?'

'Every time,' replied Jones, 'you think someone's been messing with the audit files?'

'Maybe. Do us a favour and send the boxes in my room back to archives. They're annoying Wan, who's annoying me.'

'Will do,' said the Welshman.

Mackay left the room and set off for Connaught Lane where he arrived half an hour later. He unlocked the audit cupboard and put the files out on the Boardroom table. He could see that Jonathan Bridger was not in his office and that Mrs Paterson was not at her desk. Other than the insurance issue and the discussion which would need to be had about the provisioning levels, the audit was more or less finished. As Everyman had only made £15m this year some of the provisions would have to be released and the net profit figure fudged, just as it had been every year for the last six years, but there was no way that Craven could ignore the insurance rebate.

There was a knock at the glass door and two men walked in uninvited. Mackay knew instantly that they were policemen. The shorter of the two men was the most senior. He was Teutonic looking with fairly long wavy blond hair, blue eyes and a clean cut angular jaw. He could have been thirty or forty; it was difficult to tell because of the Peter Pan like quality about him which disguised his age.

'I'm Detective Inspector Steele,' he said, 'this is Detective Sergeant Thorpe. Would you mind if we asked you a few questions?' Mackay had seen countless police dramas and he'd always wondered whether policemen introduced themselves the way they did on the telly, perhaps it was standard police procedure.

'Of course, please sit down.' They sat down and the Sergeant took out a black leather notebook. 'Any closer to tracking down the hit and run driver?' asked Mackay. The senior policeman smiled, ignored his question, and then asked his own.

'You've taken over where Mr Platt left off then Mr Mackay, anything unusual you've noticed?' Mackay wanted to run the insurance query past Craven first. His theories - on missing audit schedules, re-archived boxes, and tampered audit files - were pure speculation, and might make him look foolish if he told the police about them now without having any hard evidence. Unfortunately this briefest of hesitations was picked up by the policemen.

'No, nothing at all.' But as they looked at him disbelievingly he quickly added, 'but I haven't finished the audit yet.'

There was a long pause as the Inspector examined the auditor more closely. Mackay had very dark brown hair, almost black, which was curly in places and falling haphazardly over his brown eyes. The focal point of his face was his toothy grin, which when combined with his dark skin and swarthy looks hinted at a touch of Irish or even Romany ancestry. He was of average height and stockily built. His suit was smart enough but definitely off the peg, probably Moss Bros or the Savoy Tailors' Guild, and his shirt was poorly ironed and undone at the collar. He looked untrustworthy and he had dithered at the first question. Steele sensed that he might know something.

'Did you know Mr Platt well sir?' said the Inspector, hissing the last word and stripping it of any element of deference or politeness.

'Not really, we knew each other through work. We were colleagues rather than friends. Do you think that his death might not have been accidental?'

'No, we're treating it as a hit and run at this stage,' said the Sergeant, 'we have to investigate all possible avenues though you understand.'

'Of course,' said Mackay.

The Inspector handed Mackay a card, 'well if anything unusual should come up during your work, please call me on this number.' The policemen got up and headed for the door. The Inspector turned and looked at the seated auditor who fidgeted in anticipation of an incoming Columbo style killer question. Instead the Inspector simply said, 'anything out of the ordinary, even if it seems trivial, let me know.'

'I will,' lied Mackay.

CHAPTER 8

(FRIDAY 25TH APRIL 1997)

THE ECONOMIST BACKS MAJOR
COMPUTER GEEKS BURST INTO BLOOM
BARCLAYS BUOYANT ON BZW RUMOURS

Steadman got up early, washed, and began to shave, the procedure proving more difficult than usual because the mirror was still steamed up from Judith's earlier shower. He then dressed and headed downstairs for breakfast, picking up a copy of the Times from reception on the way. The young barman who had brought him his bar meal the previous night now acted as a waiter - Steadman knew Judith had the morning off. He glanced at the waiter who looked back at him with a sly smile. Steadman felt uncomfortable, how could this lad possibly know about last night? The young man showed him to a seat with a view over the estuary and stood ready to take his order.

'Full English please,' he snapped, and the waiter nodded and disappeared into the kitchens from where Steadman was sure he could hear stifled laughter. He opened the paper fully and looked at the headlines.

MAJOR TAKES COMMAND FOR FINAL PUSH – the battle switches to the cost of pensions.

If it was a battle, thought Steadman, then it was largely an internal one. Where the thin blue line had run out of ammo and been forced to bayonet rather than shoot each other, as Tony

Blair and his New Labour hordes looked on, ready to mop up those Tories who were still standing. Like in any apocalyptic defeat there would of course be small groups of survivors - survivors like Silas Craven - he'd only to turn up in Barnes and West Putney to get elected. The thought of Craven reminded him of his appointment at Keepers Cottage, and as it was approaching 9.45 he quickly finished his breakfast and left the Schooner.

He had passed the cottage on his way to the castle yesterday, so he easily retraced his steps and arrived punctually. Like the Dower House, the cottage was of the same dressed ochre stone that the Hall itself had been built with, and like the Dower House, had probably formed part of the original estate. The garden easily lived up to the country cottage stereotype. Although small, it was crammed full of tiny stone paths, borders and hedges. Steadman was surprised at the jumbled mass of glorious colour so early in the season, fuchsias, gladioli, and god knows what else, all jostling for space, light, and the heat of the April sun.

He battled his way along a narrow path like some latter day Chindit, but within a few seconds he was ambushed by Anne Gill, who'd been hiding behind some Oriental looking bushes. She smiled broadly at him, shook his outstretched hand, and pivoted around to the front door, beckoning him to follow her.

'Please come in Mr Steadman, do you want coffee? I take tea myself.'

'No. I mean yes. Tea will be fine.' She showed him through to a sunroom where he sat down in a comfortable old armchair. The room was glassed on three sides and was southeast facing, with northerly views to the castle and southerly views over Alnmouth and its golf course. He looked around the room and saw that Mrs Gill had all the de rigueur Miss Marple kit. Plenty of lace doilies, bits and pieces of crockery, family pictures including a wartime portrait of her husband in a RAF uniform, and all manner of useless looking knick-knacks gathered over a long lifetime. If IKEA had arrived in England, thought Steadman, it certainly hadn't reached Keepers Cottage,

Alnmouth.

She returned with a tray, complete with teapot and cosy, teacups, saucers, and some sort of heavy looking scones weighed down with large dollops of butter and scoops of whole strawberry jam.

Steadman felt a warm glow and an alien sense of nationalism sweep over him. He smiled at her as she sat down and began to pour the tea. If John Major's England of warm beer and old maidens cycling through village greens still existed anywhere - it was here, in rural Northumberland.

'I'm surprised that the garden has already come out,' he said, putting a third bite of scone into his mouth. The butter oozed between his teeth, just as it had done on his fried bread half an hour earlier. The thought of his fried breakfast and a second injection of cholesterol shortly afterwards unsettled him, and he felt the need to share his concern with Mrs Gill.

'Fried breakfast followed by buttered scones, Mrs Gill, I'm digging my grave with my knife and fork.'

'I've had butter all my life Nick,' she replied genially, 'and look at me, I'm ninety next year.'

She paused and looked out over the garden possessively before continuing.

'It's being by the coast, the garden I mean, we get a very temperate climate here.'

As if to evidence her assertion the sun appeared from behind a cloud and seemed to concentrate all of its spring warmth directly into the sunroom, compelling Steadman to take off his jacket.

'Right, Silas Craven,' she said firmly, disturbing the tranquillity of the room, 'a crook and a murderer.'

CHAPTER 9

(FRIDAY 25TH APRIL 1997 - THE SAME DAY)

Mackay was surprised that there'd been no sign of Bridger during the day and that Craven hadn't phoned him. A quick call to the office established that Sarah didn't know where Craven was, and a word with Mrs Paterson determined that Bridger had also disappeared, plus no fax had arrived from Avon and General. All in all it was a quiet day, and Mackay didn't feel like he was at the centre of a massive fraud being perpetrated on the Southern and London shareholders. He had spoken to Sally at lunchtime to tell her that he'd booked her Gibraltar ticket, and she had told him to stop imagining things. The more he thought about it, the more he became convinced that she was right. Platt had been killed by a hit and run driver, there was no seven million pound rebate, and Julie had archived the files after Platt's death.

As was usual for him on a Friday, he decided to knock off early. He threw the audit files and his briefcase into the cupboard and locked it. He took off his jacket and tie, opened his holdall and took out his jeans. He returned from the third floor toilet five minutes later transformed from City auditor to determined Sally Purcell hunter. He was fairly certain that the Everyman staff were gossiping about his early departure when he left - and he knew it was not particularly professional behaviour - but he didn't give a shit. A weekend in the sun – all expenses paid - a weekend without Commander Roper and the Cresswell Estate (although leaving the delightful Annabel to a predatory Craven was a downside) and a weekend spent with Sally Purcell. What could be more perfect?

Mackay walked to Victoria but as he wasn't due to meet Sally at the Gatwick Express until 4pm, he decided to pop into Coopers bar for a quick pint. He ordered a ropey looking bitter and sat down on one of the bar stools closest to the door. From where he was sitting he had a clear view of the entire concourse in front of him and the busy tube exit to his right. The concourse was already packed with fellow travellers who (like Mackay) had knocked off a couple of hours early to beat the weekend rush. Except that like most Fridays, because a large number of commuters all had the same idea, there was very little beating going on and quite a lot of rushing.

Mackay saw the platform number for the Brighton train called and the stationary Mass which had formed in front of the departure board took on a new shape. The Mass now lived and breathed, its behaviour completely erratic, unpredictable and above all selfish. Whilst the Mass's original semi-circular shape was maintained in skeleton form by the non-Brighton commuters, the bulk of it moved forward slowly towards the narrow gap which led onto the platform. Clearly oblivious to the huge Mass rumbling past them, the 'revenue protection officials' who had been idling about the Costa Coffee kiosk moments before, then decided to carry out a ticket inspection. This of course necessitated closing one of the two gates that guarded the gap and meant that the speed at which the Mass had been travelling was more than halved. This had the effect of bringing out the Mass's most selfish characteristics and consequently the area just in front of the gap degenerated into a melee. Mackay chuckled to himself. Other than blood sports - which was a rural activity - there was nowhere urban in a western democracy he would rather be to witness the primeval nature of man, than at Victoria station.

Mackay was distracted from his zoological observations by a man he recognised walking out of the tube exit to his right. It was the journalist he had met the previous weekend. He knocked on the window and Steadman spun round. The journalist scanned the windows of the bar, saw Mackay, half waved, stood motionless for a second, then having decided to join him, headed for the bar.

'Hi, how are you Tom,' said Steadman, 'can I get you a drink?'

'A very quick one thanks. I'm catching the Gatwick Express at 4.00. In fact I'd better have a short, make it a gin and tonic.'

Steadman went up to the bar and returned with two large G&Ts.

'Off somewhere nice for the weekend?' inquired Steadman.

'Gibraltar, my uncle died the other day and I'm an executor of his estate.' Mackay noticed that Steadman had become very animated shortly after he had begun speaking.

'Gibraltar, I can't believe it, what a coincidence.'

'What is?' said Mackay eagerly, blindly sharing the journalist's enthusiasm.

'You, going to Gibraltar. Listen, I don't mind admitting that I've been up north for the last few days checking on the background of your boss. I just arrived back at King's Cross half an hour ago and what I've heard, if true, is pretty disturbing. I'd watch out for him if I were you…er…sorry to hear about your uncle by the way.'

'You mean Silas Craven,' said Mackay, ignoring the heartfelt condolences.

'Yes. I don't have any hard evidence, but you can help me get it.'

'What's he supposed to have done?'

'If you don't mind I've got to check one or two things out first, I don't want to slander him do I? But you can help me simply by checking something out at the local paper in Gib.'

'Give us an idea,' said an intrigued Mackay, worried that his conspiracy theories were on the point of being irreversibly revived.

'All I'll say is that it involves serious criminal allegations, but I must qualify that and say again that I've no hard evidence.'

'Bloody hell,' said Mackay, thinking of Platt's death. He was tempted to mention it to Steadman but decided against it. 'Look, tell me what to look for and if I do find anything out I'll let you know - providing you agree to tell me what the allegations are first.'

'Fine,' said the journalist, pulling out a large green hard backed A4 notebook from his overnight bag. Mackay saw that the notebook had the Borough Gazette in silver letters on the top right hand corner. 'It's all in here,' continued Steadman. 'If this is true, it'll be this Administration's final scandal.'

'He's not even an MP yet,' said Mackay, 'it'll make no difference to the overall result.'

'No,' replied Steadman, 'but it'll mean the voters of Barnes and West Putney don't elect a crook.'

Steadman continued to flick through the pages of the notebook and Mackay noticed that he'd inked 'NJS' under the Gazette's lettering on the front cover, Nick J Steadman he thought.

'Here it is, Christ, I can never read my own writing, I guess being a journalist I should improve my shorthand. OK, yes, this is what she said. Craven was somehow involved with a company called the Gibraltar and Atlantic General Trading Company. My information is that it went bust in 1976 or 1977 and that he'd cooked the books for it, or at least was mixed up in it, not much to go on I know but a warmish lead.' Mackay jotted the name down in his Blake and Lander diary and finished his drink.

'No promises Nick, this won't be top of my agenda this weekend.' Steadman followed the auditor's gaze to Platform Eleven, where a shapely, attractive girl, (with discreetly highlighted and loosely bobbed hair) stood waving at them.

'I see,' said Steadman, with an understanding smile, 'well enjoy yourself and er… good luck.'

'Thanks,' said Mackay, getting up to leave, 'I will.'

Mackay skirted around the Mass and joined Sally on Platform Eleven. She looked even better from a few feet. She gave him a friendly peck on the cheek and dived into the nearest carriage which they soon discovered was almost empty.

Embarking on the Gatwick Express always had been a far more civilised affair than boarding the standard service trains. This was probably due to the more frequent service and because the Express only made one stop, however, a quick glance at the tickets reminded Mackay that the fifty percent hike in the fare might also have something to do with it.

'Who was that?' she said.

'A journalist I met at a Tory party thing last weekend - nice chap - he's doing pen portraits on all of the candidates in my constituency. You know Silas Craven is the Tory candidate.'

'Yes, I'd heard that. Will he be elected?'

'Yep. It's the sort of constituency where a hat stand wearing a blue rosette gets elected.'

'I'm surprised that you're involved with all that political stuff - never had you marked down as a party activist.'

'I'm not really, I suppose I'm a fan of Major, the Brixton Boy made good bit does impress me. I just feel that he's been badly let down by those dozen twats in his own party who had the whip withdrawn. A majority of twenty one was never enough to start with, even without ten of your own team playing offside. Who'll have heard of Eurosceptics like George Gardiner, Theresa Gorman and Richard Body in a few years time? Nobody. But the damage those Muppets have done will keep the Tories out of office for at least three terms.' Mackay checked himself, surprised at his passionate defence of the Prime Minister.

'You see, you care more than you let on. Are you pro-European?'

'I don't give a shit whether I buy my pint with a pound or a Euro. It's just a name - as long as it means we all get richer, as Europeans I mean. It has to be more sensible being able to take my ten euros out of a cash machine at Victoria and be able to spend the same ten euros in Spain, France or Greece. It's more efficient - plus it's all done without the involvement of an FX dealer in the City. I hate the way that the extortionate commission I pay enables those bastards to buy red Ferraris. We've a lot to learn from the Europeans and they have a lot to learn from us. Euroland has to be the way forward, it's the only way. I'm not saying that there aren't problems - there are huge problems - like the bloated public sectors and high taxation they have on the Continent, the common agricultural policy and outdated industrial practices. Christ, the French are on strike every other week - their lorry drivers blocking every road in France. We got rid of all that crap during the 80s and we don't want it reintroduced here via Brussels. We can teach them how to govern themselves better.'

'That's quite a tirade Tom, though you'll still not get me to vote Tory. Five years of more or less continuous sleaze, you can't defend that,' she was deliberately provoking him and it turned him on.

'I'm astonished that the media has penetrated your cynicism shield Sal, this sleaze brush that the Government's been tarred with, it's all sexual. Neil Hamilton got what, two grand in a brown envelope? The Continentals wouldn't get out of bed for a bung that size. This country probably has less corruption than anywhere else in the world. Do you know what baksheesh is?'

The term reminded her of a Rough Guide and her year out, but she couldn't remember what it was. 'I've heard of it,' she said neutrally.

'Well it's a term for institutionalised bribery - it goes on just about everywhere else in the world except on this island. And as for sexual impropriety, who gives a shit? It doesn't affect the performance of the Government.'

'Actually it does make a difference Tom,' she said, glad that they had strayed into territory which she was more familiar with, 'especially when the Government makes a point of trumpeting family values.'

'Yes, you're probably right there. I'm pretty sure Major regrets having made that Back to Basics speech. I reiterate what I said earlier though, he's been let down by his Ministers - he's pretty sleaze free himself.'

'I wouldn't bet on that,' she said thoughtfully, 'it's always the quiet ones that surprise you. There's a certain ethereal sexuality about him, it's his smile that does it. It makes you want to cuddle him. I can see some women going for him in a big way, even without the power thing.'

'Really?' said Mackay, intrigued by her insight, 'you think he might have strayed away.'

'Yep.'

'Who? Virginia Bottomley? That's what they thought on Spitting Image.'

'No, I can't see it. Besides her husband's an MP as well isn't he, difficult to see how they would get an opportunity.'

'Who else is there? There aren't many women in the Cabinet.' He paused to think. 'Gillian Shepherd?'

'What? She's Employment Secretary isn't she? I always get her confused with Edwina Currie.'

'They do look pretty similar,' agreed Mackay, remembering the Queen of Salmonella. 'No. I doubt it. I think your theory's bollocks. I just can't see 'Honest John' straying off the home patch.'

The steward with the drinks trolley arrived and interrupted their game. Mackay was glad because he fancied a drink, and besides, he was keen that Sally should start drinking early.

They arrived at the airport about forty minutes later. Mackay was surprised how busy it was. Like the earlier rail commuters, the airport travellers exhibited Mass-like characteristics, except that the airport Mass was structured into chunky gridlines emanating from the check-in desks, rather than in the unwieldy semi-circle which had formed under Victoria's departure board.

'Where are all these people going?' asked Sally, semi-rhetorically, as they joined the check-in queue.

'Don't know,' replied Mackay, 'some of them look well heeled though, and they've got a lot of stuff with them. I guess they must be fleeing the capital, the Reds are at the gate you know.' He wasn't convinced that there were many parallels between Saigon in April 1975 and Gatwick in April 1997, though he did suspect that most Daily Mail readers didn't fully understand the difference between the Vietcong and New Labour. Nevertheless, he was pleased to hear Sally laughing quietly to herself, sharing the joke.

'Yes, I think Tony Blair would look great in a huge red

neckerchief sitting astride a tank rumbling into Parliament Square.'

'With a guitar on his back of course.'

'Naturally.' They checked in, passed through security, and went into Departures.

'Don't bother getting any duty free here Sal, I remember my uncle saying that it's cheaper in Gib.'

'Ok, but I fancy doing some window shopping,' she said, scanning the rest of the lounge. She turned to face him, 'I'll meet you in that bar over there in half an hour.'

He acknowledged her instructions with three quick nods of his head and headed towards the bar.

The BA flight to Gibraltar took just under three hours. As Mackay had expected, the closer they got to Spain, the more the cloud thinned. Indeed, if he'd been in a science lab and had had the tools to plot accurately, he felt sure that he could have laid claim to some new principle of meteorology - Mackay's Law perhaps - as there seemed to be an exact correlation between the miles travelled southwards towards their destination and the reduced cloud density. And of course, by the time they approached the Rock itself, and even though it was getting dark, Mackay could see that the sky was cloudless.

The aircraft approached the Colony from the west and, as Mackay had a window seat on the starboard side of the cabin, he was well sighted to enjoy his first view of the enormous hunk of limestone which jutted almost half a kilometre out of this southerly tip of Europe. When the aircraft then banked to the right, the strip of silvery lights shining from the main town at the bottom of the rock, and further bright lights at its southerly point, gave the Rock the appearance of an enormous steel soled and steel toe capped boot - a Dr Martin perhaps - guarding the Straits of Gibraltar and kicking unwelcome visitors straight back into the Atlantic. Mackay could see that the five kilometres long Rock was sandwiched between the bay of Algeciras to the west and the Mediterranean to the East, and because of the narrow isthmus which connected it to Spain; it looked very much like an island.

Landings on runways partially reclaimed from the sea were always that bit more exciting than conventional runways, and Gibraltar was no different. As they touched down Mackay was all too aware of seawater a few feet to his right, seawater a few feet to his left and seawater just ahead of him. As the pilot wrestled with the brakes and the plane unresponsively sped closer to the Med, he furtively stole a glance at the nearest emergency exit and was sorely tempted to grab hold of Sally's hand. Not because his nerves needed steadying of course, but because comforting a young lady who was likely to be in distress was the gentlemanly thing to do.

'Must be a fairly tight landing this,' she said, with a self-assured fragility. The opportunity was too good to miss and he slipped her hand inside his and held it tightly. He was pleased when she waited for the plane to come to a complete standstill before withdrawing it.

As they got off the plane the warm air, even at that time of night, indicated that summer had already started in Gibraltar. Everyman, Bridger, Craven, Steadman, conspiracy theories, the joys of London and the beleaguered Tories - they were all a long way away - replaced instead by the potential delights of Sally Purcell.

They passed through customs and passport control quickly and then took a taxi to the Rock Hotel. It soon became apparent that their route skirted the main town, so the travellers had to make do with brief glimpses of Marks & Spencer, red post-boxes, soldiers in white pith helmets and other such signs of Britishness that the Rock was famous for. The hotel drive was extremely steep, making it difficult for the pair of auditors to clearly see what the hotel looked like as they approached it. Mackay had expected a period building with airy verandas and an atmosphere not dissimilar to the one or two gentlemen's clubs he'd visited in London. Instead, the modernish looking building was of the white, square, cubist type - typical of the early Costa Blanca style. They got out of the taxi, went into the building, and checked in. It was comfortable enough inside and had more of a colonial feel, but after they'd entered their room and opened the shutters onto their balcony, the principal strength of the hotel became apparent. Even in the half-light, they could see that the views over the bay to Spain and across the Straits of Gibraltar to Morocco (and the Atlas mountains) were simply stunning.

'This is great,' she said, 'let's leave the unpacking and head down for dinner, it's already late.'

They both ordered shellfish for starters and steaks for the main course. They were the last to order and Mackay saw that most of their fellow diners were nearing the end of their meals. This meant that they not only had two waiters all to themselves, but also the entire kitchen staff solely devoted to the preparation of their food. Mackay felt that they were in danger of finishing too quickly, and more importantly, before he'd had an opportunity to order the second bottle of wine.

There was still a third of the first bottle left when the steaks arrived, so he took a large gulp out of his own glass, refilled it, and crammed as much as he could into Sally's - merging the meniscus and top of the wineglass into one. She took a sip out of it, but it was too full and wine dribbled enticingly down her chin.

'Are you trying to get me pissed?' she said.

'Course not,' lied Mackay forcefully, 'shall we have another bottle?' He could see from her face that he'd been too premature. Perhaps he shouldn't have consulted her and just ordered it anyway, either way, it was too late.

'I think this one will do Tom, I've plenty here.' Mackay began to nurse his own drink, resigned to the fact that his quest wouldn't be aided by the second bottle.

The restaurant was empty apart from a group of elderly Germans, who had massed, unsurprisingly, at the best tables nearest to the windows. The largest of these Germans, clean shaven, balding, very fat, and wearing a loose fitting blue shirt in the Hawaiian style, was Klaus. Mackay knew his name was Klaus, because a couple of minutes earlier the head waiter had arrived at Klaus's table with a large birthday cake and a chorus of Happy Birthday (in English) had soon followed. It turned out that Klaus was eighty. And if the dozen or so Germans had been boisterous before the arrival of the cake and their spirited rendition of Happy Birthday, then they were positively noisy afterwards. Klaus had schnapps with his wife, schnapps with his fellow Germans, schnapps with the head waiter, schnapps with the other waiters, and the chef (who had no doubt baked the cake) was summoned from the kitchen and given schnapps. And finally, just as Mackay was finishing his glass of wine, he became aware of a large blue Hawaiian shirt heading in his direction.

'You will have some schnapps with me,' said the German, looking at Sally.

'Yes, of course I will,' replied the English Rose, gulping down the remainder of her wine. Klaus then tipped the bottle upside down and the schnapps splashed freely into their empty glasses, filling them half way. 'To you Klaus,' she said.

'Down in one, after three,' insisted the octogenarian German, filling up his own thimble sized schnapps glass, 'one, two, three.' The three of them downed their drinks, unused to the burning liquid Sally gasped, and Mackay stifled a girly cough.

'Bloody hell,' he gasped, 'Happy Birthday.'

'Cheers,' said the beaming German. Who turned, slowly round, in much the same way that steam locomotives used to on railway turntables, and then headed back to his friends.

'Well I'm up for a party now Tom,' said the flushed auditoress, 'our fellow Europeans have given me a bit of a buzz. Shall we get another bottle, or do you fancy heading out?'

'Let's skip dessert and head into Town.'

'OK,' she replied, putting her napkin on to the table, 'let's go.'

The beauty of full board of course was that you just got up and left when you'd finished. There was no need to catch the waiter's eye, ask for the bill and then hang around for ten minutes whilst he found it. Then, after you'd checked it and attached your card to it, catch his eye again, and then wait a further ten minutes for him to put it through the machine. Some waiters, who were likely to be French or Italian students working on the Kings Road, had developed this dawdling technique into an art form. Naturally being Continental, they were the gastronomic superior to those whom they were serving, so it was only right that they should keep customers waiting when they were keen to leave. Instead of dealing with this usual faff, the auditors were soon walking through reception, down the hotel's steep drive, and after a short walk, they were ensconced in the Gibraltar Arms on Main Street.

They talked and drank, and drank and talked, until they were both drunk. It was well after midnight when Sally noticed that the pub was empty and that the barman had began putting stools on top of the bar.

'I feel like your mistress Tom,' she said. 'All expenses paid weekend to the sun, great hotel, great food, loads of booze - still waiting for the expensive jewellery though.' She paused. 'And not a single thought of my deceased boyfriend.'

'Let's face it, he was pretty bloody dull,' slurred Mackay.

There was a long silence as they both thought of Platt. Mackay spoke first.

'Getting back to the mistress bit,' he said, with a dirty smile.

'What of it?' she replied with faked innocence.

'Of course being a mistress brings with it certain obligations, as well as the benefits you just mentioned.'

'What obligations might they be, kind sir,' she said mischievously, fluttering her eyelids.

'Sexual obligations,' he said firmly. They looked at each other and he reached forward and kissed her. She responded, but pulled back when the impatient barman deliberately clattered some chairs.

'Well, if it's my duty as a mistress,' she said, with mock resentment, swaying slightly as she got to her feet, 'we'd better get on with it.'

'Bloody hell,' said Mackay for the second time that evening, leaping from his chair.

The journey back to the hotel seemed all too long and the

drive up all too steep as the lusty number crunchers staggered, lurched, and giggled their way back to their hotel room. As Mackay lay on the bed alone, he was concerned that he might have had *too* much to drink and that this might soon cause a devastating physical problem, however, the sight of Sally bolting naked from behind the bathroom door soon demonstrated that these fears were unwarranted.

Mackay wasn't quite sure what or where nirvana was, but he knew that that sunny Saturday in Gibraltar got pretty close to it. To begin with, the happy bean counters took the cable car to the Top of the Rock and flirted publicly with each other whilst enjoying the views. Then they showed a flagrant disregard for rules and regulations and fed the Barbary Apes. After that they visited St Michael's Cave and talked loudly during a guided tour. Then they played at Spanish invaders and British defenders in the O'Hara battery. And finally, when they couldn't hold on any longer, they skipped merrily down the Mediterranean Steps back to their hotel room and spent the rest of the afternoon and early evening in bed.

'What a lovely day Tom,' said Sally, yawning. It had been an active day.

'Interesting what that guide told us today, I mean about Gibraltar's history,' he said, flicking through a newly acquired guide book and only half hearing her, fortunately his sensors picked up the need to react and he kicked into auto-response, 'er.... yes, cracking day Sal, same again tomorrow.' He left enough of a pause before returning to his original topic, and then continued. 'I must confess that I always thought that the reason the folk on this Rock didn't want to hook up again with Spain was because they all know how good they've got it here. Low taxes, virtually duty free goods, plus having the UK's muscle when you need it, it's a good deal. They had a valid argument twenty odd years ago, and although I claim to be a right-winger, I wouldn't have fancied living in Franco's Spain - but now, it's different.'

'You've confused me, are you saying that they should be

joined back up with Spain, or not?'

'Not. It's the historical context you see - they don't feel any more Spanish than you or I do. It was like that guide was saying today in the Cave, up until…when was it…' Mackay consulted his guidebook. '…1462, the Rock was controlled by the Moors, and over there wasn't even called Spain, the Moors called it al-Andalus. So when the British arrived in 1713 the Spanish had only been here for about 250 years, whereas the British have now been here for nearly 300 years already. Plus the Spanish still have their enclaves in Morocco. What did he say they were called? Ceuta, and something…'

'…Melilla, I think it was.'

'Right. No wonder folk here are a bit concerned about Thursday. Can't see the wishes of thirty thousand or so non-voting colonists cutting much ice in Milbank, even if they did help us in our hour of greatest need.'

'No,' said Sally thoughtfully. 'Colony and imperial aren't words you're likely to find in New Labour jargon.' She rolled over to his side of the bed and ran her hands through his hair. 'You think you don't care but you're more of a political animal than you realise.' She paused. 'But we've had nothing but politics for the last month and I'm sick of it. Give me that guide, and *I'll* decide what we're doing tomorrow.'

The Sunday was much the same as the Saturday, except that the sights were different. They first visited the Moorish castle and its keep the Tower of Homage. And then the spectacular fourteenth century Moorish baths which were incorporated into the Gibraltar museum. On their way to Europa Point, the most southerly part of the European mainland, they stopped off at the Trafalgar Cemetery where those who had survived the French and the Spanish were brought onshore to be killed off by Royal Navy surgeons.

'Look at this one Sal,' said Mackay, pointing to one of the few readable headstones, *'Lieutenant, William Forster, late of his Majesty's Ship Colossus, died of the wounds he received in the glorious battle of Trafalgar, the 21 day of October 1805, aged 20.'*

'Poor lad,' said Sally. 'I bet 'died of his wounds' covers all manner of medical incompetence and unsanitary conditions.'

They continued on foot for about half an hour in a southerly direction, passing the naval base, commercial docks and numerous decaying Second World War military buildings.

'It's in a bit of a time warp this place,' said Mackay, as they passed a huge dilapidated green building which looked like it might once have been a hospital. 'I'm surprised that the Tories haven't tried to sell some of this lot off - there's a lot of empty real estate here.'

'Maybe the Yanks have told them to hang onto it and the MOD is getting a bung for doing so.'

They reached Europa Point twenty minutes later sweating profusely. Mackay regretted not having taken a hat, Sally regretted the lack of a water bottle and they both regretted their decision to walk for an hour in the blazing midday sun. Looking out across the Straits, Mackay noted from his guide book that there'd been a naval base there since Phoenician times. He could see why. The strategic importance of the Rock was obvious. Any unwelcome shipping passing through this gateway to the Mediterranean could be blasted, either by warships or by the huge batteries behind him. He saw now that in the age of sea power, as well as the best ships and the best sailors, the best navy had needed the best bases. This was why the Rock had been in the hands of the Royal Navy for nearly 300 hundred years.

'Well here we are Sal,' said Mackay, clumsily putting his arms around her in an attempt to create a romantic moment, 'the Continent doesn't go any further south, we're at the end of Europe.'

'That ain't true young fella,' came a loud American voice from behind them. 'There's a place called Tarifa over there on the Spanish mainland which is further south.'

Mackay looked round and saw that the voice of the smart alec cum slayer of romantic moments fitted the stereotype. The man was close to crossing the boundary between very fat and obese. He wore a white linen shirt which was somehow tucked into his beige tailored shorts. On his head, he had the obligatory white baseball cap, with the letters US splashed in large red letters on the front of it, just in case he forgot his own nationality. Mackay decided to play the imperialist and looked directly at the man, lifted the tip of his nose, stuck out his chin, and narrowed his eyes.

'Really,' he said in his best Kenneth Williams voice, then turning to Sally he continued 'you know dear, those Americans were never very good at geography, come along now.' With that he guided her back towards the town, and as they waited at the bus stop, the helpful American passed them in a gleaming rented Range Rover and waved.

CHAPTER 10

(MONDAY 28TH APRIL 1997)

TORY BIG GUNS TURN ON CURRIE
ST TRINIANS TO RETURN WITH SPICE GIRL POWER
GOLDEN YEARS COME FLOODING BACK AS ARMS PARK PREPARES FOR BULLDOZERS

The firm of Likudi, Benady, Gomez and Scott, Solicitors, was located on Linewall Road, which Mackay found without difficulty the following day. He saw that all the buildings on Linewall Road were old, and the building belonging to the legal representatives of his deceased uncle was no exception. The structure had three storeys, was probably Georgian and had the obligatory brass plaque with the partners' names inscribed on it. He noticed that the first name on the plaque was John Benady, Mr Likudi presumably having reached the lucrative, yet undemanding, semi-retired stage of consultant. The entrance to number 8B Linewall Road was through a set of large blue double doors with the '8' on the left hand door and the 'B' on the right. Mackay soon discovered that only the right hand door opened. He went inside and was shown to a waiting room. The look, feel, and atmosphere of the office felt like that of some expanding provincial legal practice, probably in the Home Counties, but it wasn't, it wasn't quite English.

At 9.00 he was shown into the room of the Senior Partner, who sat behind a large mahogany desk with a green leather inlay. There was a vast quantity of weighty legal tomes, digests and law reports crammed onto every shelf in the room - each book no doubt very important and each book no doubt written in that legal speak which lawyers are at pains to ensure that no layman can understand. Like his offices, John Benady was English but somehow not English. English was obviously his native tongue - but the way he spoke, his accent, the words he used - wasn't quite English. He didn't look English, but then again he didn't look Spanish. His skin was dark, darker than Mackay's, but his eyes were bright blue, almost Nordic looking.

'I trust you're enjoying your stay on the Rock,' he said smoothly after their introductions, 'did you bring your wife with you?'

'Yes, well my… er… girlfriend actually. I've sent her to Main Street to get some duty free.' Was she his girlfriend? He liked the idea of it, but suspected that she wouldn't see it the same way. The solicitor pulled open a draw on his desk and handed him a card.

'If you wish to purchase duty free, I suggest you try here, Mr Mackay. Your goods will cost half the price of Main Street. Main Street is just for the…' he paused, deliberating carefully over his next word, '…tourists. Please mention my name to the proprietor and you may get an additional discount.'

'Thanks very much,' said Mackay.

'Don't mention it. I was very fond of your Uncle. I spent many a long evening with him at his villa, and as a consequence I'll always associate mornings there with a sore head.' He paused, and Mackay sensed that he was smiling internally. 'And now to business, your Uncle was a man of some estate.'

The accountant and the lawyer then spent the next three hours pouring over the will, probate documents and assets and liabilities. By lunchtime Mackay began to feel that the trip had started to look like a busman's holiday and he was concerned at how his Uncle's liabilities had mounted up. From mortgages here and undischarged bank loans there, to unpaid grocery and utility bills, all in all creditors were owed just over five hundred grand - but the assets were larger. Mackay had hoped that there might be some way that he and his sister could hang onto his Uncle's villa - a light, spacious, beautifully converted former water mill in Jimenez de la Frontera, a mountain village about twenty miles inland. But being the principal asset, and valued at over a million pounds, this had proved unrealistic, especially as he knew that his cousins had no interest in it and would prefer the cash. There was also a small flat in St John's Wood, and the balance was made up of cash, government bonds and equities. Benady was also in favour of retaining the villa in Jimenez but for different reasons.

'Of course your Uncle never fully disclosed all of his financial affairs to me,' began Benady, with a lawyer's usual disclaimer of liability, 'so I couldn't swear to the fact that all the money your Uncle used to purchase the villa, was.....er.....taxed.'

He paused to study Mackay's reaction, which seemed to pass the test, because he then continued in the same vein as before.

'Also, given that your Uncle wasn't tax resident in the UK, and that he hadn't lived in the UK for some years, one might argue that he'd lost his UK domesticity for inheritance tax purposes. On that basis, and considering that the property *is* in Spain, it might be reasonably argued that the villa, for the Inland Revenue's purposes, shouldn't form part of his estate. In fact, perhaps there's no need to disclose the existence of the villa to them at all.' He stopped and looked closely at Mackay again, who looked back at him with a blank expression.

Mackay had failed his tax exams on several occasions and when four years ago he'd eventually passed them, it would have been fair *then* to describe his tax knowledge as patchy. Now he simply knew nothing, except that he did remember that the golden rule was that you never hid anything from the taxman, and that those who did, had something to hide and did so at their peril.

'But wouldn't the villa have to be somehow taxed in Spain?' he asked neutrally. Mackay wasn't interested in the solicitor's response because it was clear to him that after his Uncle's business, Sharp's Motors, had been sold, Benady had in some way helped his uncle bring some, if not all, of the untaxed proceeds into Spain. Knowing his uncle, this would probably have been using a suitcase full of cash. Whatever the method was, it was plain that Benady felt a little exposed.

'Yes, maybe a little tax,' said Benady, encouraged by Mackay's question, 'but it's easier to make it disappear over here where there are more loopholes and grey areas.'

Mackay was a professional, and professionals didn't defraud the Revenue - not illegally anyway. Of course he knew that the partners at Blake and Lander paid less tax than a bin man, but the advantage of having the very best tax advice was that there were countless legal dodges, tricks, and avoidance measures that could be employed to avoid a liability. And unlike FT-SE 100 directors, who had every detail of their remuneration packages crawled over by analysts, but whom often received less than their auditors, all of it was neatly hidden behind the veil of the partnership structure. Mackay knew that it would be to his personal benefit to hide the villa from the Revenue. If it could be done by bending the rules then he was up for it, but there was a difference between bending and breaking, and this sounded like breaking. At the moment though he was keen to keep the solicitor on side, and his instinct told him not to knock back the lawyer's help, not at this stage anyway.

'Sounds like it should be something we should consider John,' he said collaboratively, 'let me think about it over the next few days.'

'Good idea,' said Benady enthusiastically, certain that his scheme had been adopted by Mackay. 'Even if we don't go ahead with this I suggest that you set up a personal bank account here in Gibraltar. There may be some other bits and pieces which can be usefully kept off-shore and remitted back to the UK at your leisure, depending on your own tax circumstances in any one particular year. I can sort this out within a day or two. I tend to use the Gibraltar and West Mediterranean Bank, or the GWM as we call it. I have the forms here if you'd care to sign them now.'

Mackay signed the forms and handed them back to the solicitor. 'Well that's about everything. I'll be in touch during

the week to finalise our options.'
'There's one other thing John.'
'What is it?'
'A friend of mine, a journalist, is doing an article on an election candidate who may have been mixed up in some scandal over here in the 1970s.'
'Well, I was a young man,' said Benady, with a genuine smile, 'try me.'
'I think it was something to do with the Gibraltar and Atlantic General Trading Company.'
'Yessss,' replied the lawyer, drawing out the s sound and at the same time doing a fair impression of Jeremy Paxman. 'We don't have many scandals in Gibraltar - or many unnatural deaths - but a scandal and an unnatural death are most unusual.'
'Really,' said the intrigued auditor, 'please go on.'
Benady sat back in his chair, rotated about ninety degrees clockwise so that he could see out of the window across the bay to Spain, and then continued. 'Couldn't tell you exactly when it was, late 1975 or early 1976, it was certainly around about then. I know because Franco had just died and that was part of the problem. You must remember Tom that although relations with Spain are always a bit strained, even now, in the 70s it was completely different. With the border closed we really felt like we were in a state of siege, and as a consequence things were a little less civilised than they are today. Some entrepreneurs thought that the death of Franco would bring opportunities and would mean that the border would be opened, so many of them speculated, buying warehouses and property near the border crossing, investing in stock, generally preparing for the gates to open. Of course 1975 turned into 1976 and there had been no change. Then 1976 became 1977 and so on, until 1985, when it eventually did open. But by then a lot of people had gone bust and Peter Vassallo was one of them. He was the MD of the Gibraltar and Atlantic General Trading Company which had taken the biggest punt of all and had borrowed heavily. He was a popular local businessman,

well connected with officials in Franco's regime. He'd had one or two grocery stores both sides of the border, nothing big, and so looking back it was surprising that he'd gambled so heavily on this one venture and that he'd got the finance to do it. As time went on, and as his stock sat rotting in his warehouses the other side of the border, things must have become fairly desperate. But amazingly his bank continued to prop him up and he limped on for months. No one was really surprised when he fell to his death off the top of the Rock - suicide they said.'

'But that's not what you think John.'

'Well, off the record, I remember thinking to myself at the time that it was all a bit too neat. Why would he have punted so much on such a risky venture? He must've had a tip off from someone in Madrid, but then there must have been a change of plan which caught him out.'

'You don't think it was suicide.'

'Spanish secret service would be my guess, pushed him off the top of the Rock to shut him up, maybe he was planning to take a few others with him when his company crashed.' Benady then checked himself, suddenly aware that he'd left that comfortable, traditional, safe, conservative world inhabited only by lawyers, and wandered into the realms of fantasy and espionage. 'Of course, this is all pure speculation on my part Tom, probably all a load of nonsense.'

'I'm sure you're right,' said Mackay, 'you wouldn't happen to remember who the company's bankers were by any chance.'

'Fraid not, it *was* a long time ago. Listen I'm no corporate lawyer but if you're that interested try the library, they keep all sorts of stuff down there, statutory records, accounts, company filings, that sort of thing.'

'I might just do that. Thanks again for your time,' said Mackay, as if it had been free.

'I'll call you later in the week to finalise what we discussed earlier,' said Benady.

They shook hands at the large blue double doors, the solicitor smiling broadly at his fellow professional as he turned to exit the building. Mackay smiled back and then headed towards Main Street. He could easily see why his Uncle had chosen Benady as his lawyer. He could imagine the pair of old rogues sitting on the veranda at Jimenez, drinking cerveza, smoking large, completely excise free Cuban cigars and devising all manner of barely legal schemes. He had liked him.

He found Sally loitering around Marks & Spencer. Fortunately she hadn't yet bought any duty free and he told her about Benady's 'locals only' warehouse. He then passed on what Benady had told him about the Gibraltar and Atlantic General Trading Company, and she suggested that they went to the library immediately.

The library, or Garrison Library as it was known, was a fine-looking early nineteenth century building and former officers' club situated on Governor's Parade. The would-be detectives were pleased to discover that the building also doubled up as the offices of the Gibraltar Chronicle, which was handy for the pair, considering that they were to spend most of the afternoon going through the newspaper's archives.

'I guess your journalist friend had dud information,' said Sally, looking at her watch. Their flight was at 5 pm and she was keen that they were on their way. 'C'mon Sherlock, we'd better get back to the hotel and pick up the bags, London's calling.'

'This is all I've found Sal,' said Mackay, holding out a browning dog eared document and a newspaper cutting, 'it just really confirms what we suspected already.'

'What is it?' she inquired.

'It's the Gibraltar and Atlantic General Trading Company's last set of filed accounts. According to these the company was in great shape and had substantial net assets. We now know of course that these stock figures which are shown in the balance sheet are Mickey Mouse, and guess who the auditors were?'

'Are you about to say Blake and Lander,' said Sally.

'Almost, remember this was twenty years ago, try Blake and Scott. We might be able to find out who the partner was when we get back to the office, I bet it's Craven. Now guess who the company's bankers were?'

'Would I be mistaken if I said the Southern and London Bank?'

'No, you wouldn't. The relationship manager has to be Jonathan Bridger. He even told me that he'd been posted to Gib back in the 70s.'

'So there could be a link,' she said, sounding unconvinced. 'What does the newspaper cutting say?'

'It's a report of the inquest into Peter Vassallo's death, a suicide verdict was recorded, but the hack who penned this sounds unconvinced.

Gibraltar Chronicle *7 May 1977*

Local businessman plunges 300 metres to death to avoid fraud probe

The inquest into the death of local businessman Peter Vassallo recorded a verdict of suicide yesterday. The coroner, Mr Joe Karm, heard evidence that Mr Vassallo, whose company had been experiencing severe financial difficulties, was having a meal in the Mons Calpe restaurant with business associates on the evening of 8 April when he had become depressed. The restaurant manager, Mr Lorenzo Cachia, testified that Mr Vassallo had been drinking heavily and had been 'difficult' on several occasions during the evening. The Coroner heard how Mr Cachia had seen Mr Vassallo get up from his table after an altercation with one of his associates, and say that he needed some air. Mr Karm was satisfied that Mr Vassallo had then taken his own life. In his summing up, the Coroner said that his conclusions had been heavily influenced by the police investigation into Mr Vassallo's business affairs which had commenced shortly after his death. The Police had concluded that it was likely that Mr Vassallo's company had been trading fraudulently for some time, and it was possible that Mr Vassallo had personally defrauded the company, the company's creditors, and its shareholders.

After the court had adjourned, Mr Karm refused to answer questions as to why the two business associates of Mr Vassallo hadn't given evidence in court, and why the police report into the fraud at the Gibraltar and Atlantic General Trading Company hadn't been published.

'Interesting,' said Sally, 'there's the photocopier, you copy, I'll cab hail, we'll pick up the bags and drop in at your solicitor's bonded warehouse on the way out to the airport. There's no way I'm missing out on a two quid litre bottle of Gordon's.'

CHAPTER 11

(MONDAY 28TH APRIL 1997 - THE SAME DAY)

Mackay got back to his flat at 7.30 and straight away noticed how tidy it was. This concerned him, because he knew that there was no way that Ed could achieve such a high level of cleanliness on his own. It could only mean that Atif had been in Putney all weekend, instead of visiting his girlfriend in Leeds, like he was supposed to do. As Atif went north every weekend without fail, Mackay was worried that something was amiss.

'Good weekend you Arab?' said Mackay, with false confidence, cautiously entering the lounge. Mackay had long ago acknowledged Atif as the world's worst Muslim and Atif had been happy and honoured to wear the crown, but it was unusual even for the world's worst Muslim to be tucking into an enormous scotch on a Monday night.

'She's dumped me Tomboy,' came the predictable reply, 'for a van driver from Pontefract, one of the little people.' Mackay couldn't help laughing. Atif was pure Pakistani aristocracy who'd arrived in London as an undergraduate in the late 80s and had never gone home. Mackay had never met a bigger snob, for him to be dislodged by 'one of the little people,' as he termed the inhabitants of socio-economic groups D and E, was hilarious.

'Come off it,' said Mackay, 'it's not as if you and Tracy were exactly matched. You were only shagging her because you can't get near any of your own women.'

'Tracy and I had a lot in common,' he said, with an attempt at seriousness. 'We shared culture, the arts, philosophy, we were kindred spirits. I'll never get over the loss.' At this Atif burst out laughing, and proceeded to pour a substantial whisky into the empty tumbler which Mackay suspected had been placed by the bottle in anticipation of his arrival.

'Perhaps you'll bugger off back to your own country now and leave our women to us.'

'Oh yeah, I forgot how successful you were on your home patch, Tomboy. By the way, how are you getting on with the lovely Annabel?'

'She's yesterday's news Mustapha.' As Atif's hairline had begun to recede quite dramatically, Mackay had taken to calling him Mustapha, or to give him his full Sunday name, Mustapha Wig. 'Now, let me tell you about *my* weekend,' continued the auditor. He then told Atif about his dirty weekend in Gibraltar, highlighting the comfortable attractions of Miss Sally Purcell, sparing none of the detail and embellishing wherever possible. When Mackay had finished, Atif forced out a loud and lengthy artificial yawn.

'So you're not interested in Annabel anymore then?'

'Not in the slightest,' replied Mackay haughtily.

'I'll just delete this message on the answer phone then,' said Atif, feigning to get up and head for the phone.

'That won't be necessary,' said Mackay with a smile, picking up his drink and heading for the hall. He pressed the play button and listened.

'Tom, its Annabel Mylner,' she sounded very excited and it was clear that she was in a hurry, 'and it's...Monday at just gone six... sorry to hear about your uncle, Roper told me about it - we missed you this weekend. It's not good news I'm afraid, our local poll result came out on Friday and I think this seat may have become a marginal - we're all in a state of shock. We're only two points ahead of Labour and three points ahead of the LibDems. Silas has been wonderful, very calm. He said that there's no way that Barnes and West Putney would ever fall. The Borough Gazette's even come out against us - it must be that horrible little man from the debate the other night.

They're hinting that Silas isn't suitable to be an MP. Silas says that after Thursday he's going to sue them, but at the moment he doesn't want to rock the boat. I know that you've probably been travelling all day but can you come round, we're all in a flap here, we've got an important visitor coming, quite unexpected. Listen, I've got to go, hope to see you later, bye.' The message ended and Mackay finished his drink.

'I'm off Atif,' he shouted through to the lounge, 'duty calls.'

'Tomboy,' came the reply.

'What?' said the auditor, putting his hand on the front door latch.

'I've decided to vote Labour.'

'But you're a bloody toff!' Then he paused for a moment thinking aloud, 'anyway, who said you're allowed to vote?' Mackay realised that he was being wound up. So he hurled a sharp 'Piss off Mustapha' in Atif's general direction, opened the door, ignored the 'Fuck off you Imperialist' response which emanated from the lounge and set off in the direction of Balfour Street.

He could feel the effects of the whisky as he rounded the corner and approached the nerve centre of the Barnes and West Putney Conservative party. He was surprised to see a large noisy crowd gathered outside the building and what appeared to be some TV cameras and several journalists milling around. He noticed that since his last visit the occupants of the second floor flat above the Tanning Shop had stuck a large, 'Vote Labour,' poster in their front window. Mackay was sorry to have missed the look on Roper's face when that had gone up. He entered the building and met the agent in the hallway.

'Thanks very much for coming Tom,' said the Commander quickly, grabbing his arm. 'Hope everything went OK in Gibraltar? Would you mind being part of a supportive crowd and cheering when our visitor comes out of the building with Silas? There are plenty of rosettes, placards and things in my room, Annabel will sort you out.'

'Will do Lawrence,' replied Mackay, 'just got to pop into the little boys' room first.'

Mackay went into the toilet and saw the Prime Minister standing at the left urinal. Mackay sidled up beside him and began pissing into the urinal next to him. The noise of the crowd outside and the clamour of the party workers within the building had failed to reach the interior of the Balfour Street Gentlemens', so other than the sound of gently trickling liquid, it was strangely quiet and peaceful.

After a few moments, Mr Major finished urinating but continued to stand facing the wall. Mackay sensed a Prime Ministerial unwillingness to go back out into the happy throng - the Balfour Street Gentlemens' providing the Brixton Boy with a brief respite from the multitude.

Mackay finished his own business and walked over to the washbasins where the party leader soon joined him. He turned to him and saw the man behind the public face. Seven difficult years in office had left their mark, he looked absolutely knackered.

The pair of Tories continued to wash their hands in an awkward silence. Mackay looked at the PM again, and he looked back at him. As if they were somehow joined at the hip they then moved in unison to the only paper towel dispenser, Mackay got there first, but he attempted to pull too many towels through the gap and they got stuck.

Mackay had been staring, and he suddenly became aware that the First Lord of the Admiralty was staring back at him, somewhat embarrassed he then said the first thing which popped into his head.

'Election going well then is it?'

The Prime Minister's eyes twinkled, the corners of his mouth quivered, and he began to giggle, then he giggled some more, then the giggle became a chuckle, which soon became a laugh, and within a few seconds the pair of Tories were roaring with laughter.

'Very...very...very ...,' said Mr Major, unable to continue because he was laughing so much, 'very well thanks.'

As the bizarre hilarity of the moment began to subside,

Mackay studied him more closely and saw that the burdens of office were gradually slipping from him. Here was a man more than anyone else looking forward to Friday morning - he simply couldn't give a shit anymore.

'Well if things don't go to plan…' said Mackay mischievously, '…why not ignore the result? Give the generals a call today and make sure they're on side, I'm happy to set up a few barricades across Westminster Bridge on Friday morning if you want.'

'OK,' said the MP. 'I'll ask Norma to remind me to bring my pitchfork down from Huntingdon.'

'Are you ready Prime Minister?' bellowed a loud voice from the other side of the door.

'Seriously though,' said Mackay, as Mr Major moved towards the exit. 'Good luck on Thursday.'

'Luck's got nothing to do with it my friend,' said the Prime Minister, turning back to face Mackay with a genuine smile. 'We're fucked!'

CHAPTER 12

(TUESDAY 29TH APRIL 1997)

72 HOURS TO SAVE UNION SAYS MAJOR
NEW TAIL IN THE LIFE OF HAIL-BOPP
NEW GOALKEEPER IS A GIVEN FOR NEWCASTLE

Mackay arrived early at Connaught Lane. He went up to the third floor and having got out the files from the locked cupboard, settled himself behind the Boardroom table. Everything was just as he'd left it the previous Friday. He called Sarah, but just for a change she didn't know where Craven was or when he'd be in. Then he called the offices of the Borough Gazette and was told that there was no sign of Steadman, and that nobody knew where he was. Added to this he'd seen that Bridger wasn't about and Mrs Paterson didn't know where he was either.

'Pretty difficult doing an audit without a director or a partner, June,' he said jokingly to Bridger's secretary.

'Yes, he's not been in much lately,' agreed Mrs Paterson, 'must be something to do with the merger.'

'Do you know if those policemen have made any progress in finding the hit and run driver yet?' inquired Mackay.

'Not that I've heard…,' she broke off as the Boardroom phone rang and Mackay went to get it.

He picked up the receiver and said in his best phone voice, 'good morning Blake and Lander, Tom Mackay speaking.' He'd expected to hear Craven's clipped voice on the other end of the line but instead he was forced to move the phone away from his ear as the noise coming from the other end was deafening.

'You anglicised bastard Mackay - you gone completely native now,' said the voice in a soft but loud Edinburgh accent, an accent which Mackay thought sounded more English than the speaker would care to admit. 'I knew you'd sell out to the English at the first opportunity.'

'What do you want Rab?' said Mackay apprehensively.

'What, no how are you Rab? What've you been up to Rab? When are you coming down to see me Rab?'

'What do you want Rab?' repeated Mackay.

'Well, now that you ask I'm in London on Wednesday and wondered whether you could put me up. I've got some dreary compliance conference at the Barbican during the day and I fancy a night out in the Smoke. What you doing?'

'Well in case you hadn't noticed there's a general election on Thursday and I've been charged with saving the nation from being overrun by the Reds. I can meet you for a quick drink in town but that's about it. Of course you're welcome to stay but don't trash the place this time. You still got your key?'

'On a gold chain around my neck Tommy Boy.'

'What's the political mood like in Edinburgh by the way?'

'Hilarious,' replied Rab. 'Forsyth rarely ventures out of his St Andrew's House bunker, and when he does sortie out to proclaim doom and gloom about the Tartan Tax, he has to scurry back again sharpish to avoid a lynch mob. The Tories will be wiped out up here I reckon.'

'How's the fund management game?' asked Mackay, 'still fleecing honest folks who are trying to save for their retirement and still charging them large fees to lose their money.'

'God you're a cynic Thomas,' replied the compliance officer. 'How can we be responsible for unpredictable market movements or senior management failings? Besides, the fees which we levy are very reasonable and naturally allow fund managers and myself to continue to enjoy the sort of lifestyle to which we've become accustomed. Okay, if you'd invested a thousand pounds with us two years ago it might only be worth six hundred now, but remember you need to benchmark this return against the North Korean Bearer Bond Index. Compared to that, our performance was stellar.'

'Bloody Hell,' said Mackay, 'you almost sound as if you believe your own PR. Christ, your snouts are deeper in the City trough than both the analysts and investment bankers put together. Your job *is* to spot unpredictable market movements and bad management, that's why you're paid so handsomely.'

'Come come Tom, you can't really expect us to return our fees if we lose other people's money, you'll be asking us to get rid of our darts boards next.'

'Good day to you Mr Anderson,' continued Mr Mackay. 'I hope you choke on your in-flight lobster and Krug on the way down.'

Mackay hung up. Despite getting a Third, Rab had somehow blundered his way into compliance just as it was becoming fashionable. BCCI and Barings had increased demand for trained buffoons like him and this need was likely to continue as long as Executives felt tempted to put their fingers in the till. Rab was happy to jump on the gravy train just like everybody else, but his defence of the fund management industry wasn't serious. On the few occasions when Mackay *had* met actual Fund Managers, both through Rab and via his audit work, he'd been astonished to discover that despite regularly losing other people's money, they all believed that they added value. Mackay farted loudly. The thought of Rab and his blood-sucking colleagues had been enough to move his bowel, so without delay he headed for the third floor gents.

When he returned he saw that Bridger was at his desk with his back to the door, talking on the phone. By the time Mackay had himself sat down, the banker had started another call which Mackay immediately realised was to one of those new telephone banks.

'Jonathan Bridger,' came the voice from next door. '7th May 1945. Little Mill, East Chirnside, Kelso, Roxburghshire. Yes, the account number is 763821.'

Now for the password thought Mackay. He knew that

Bridger had two children, Steven and Yvette, and that his wife's name was Virginia. Would a security conscious banker choose a family name as a password?

'V,' said Bridger.

Had Mackay guessed right?

'E,' continued the banker.

So that cuts out his wife thought the amateur sleuth.

'T.'

There was a long pause as the other caller confirmed the accuracy of the verification. This was accepted and Bridger gave instructions to move £100,000 to another account. Mackay's immediate thought was that this sum formed part of the insurance rebate and that Bridger, sensing that the net was closing in, was moving it off-shore. The phone rang in the Boardroom and Mackay picked it up.

'Blake and Lander,' he said, and as he spoke Bridger spun round in his chair and looked directly at him questioningly through the glass partition. He looked back at Bridger and held his stare. 'Did you hear my phone call?' was in Bridger's eyes. 'I might have,' was in Mackay's.

'Tom, are you still there?' It was Erica Quirke.

'Yes,' he replied curtly, his gaze still fixed on Bridger.

'That fax you were after has arrived. What do you want me to do with it?'

He used the opportunity of picking up Everyman's internal phone book to break off Bridger's stare. He found the fax number for the Credit Department and gave Erica the number. It was too risky to use the fax outside the Boardroom which he shared with Bridger.

'Oh, one other thing Tom.'

'What?'

'Your archived box mystery from the other day.'

'Yes.'

'Jules is certain she didn't send the boxes back.'

'Thanks Erica. Bye.'

He sensed Bridger swing round in his chair and face his desk. What will he do now thought Mackay? Does he know what

I'm up to? Just then he heard a fax phone ringing across the room in the Credit Department. He immediately got up and casually walked across the floor. He saw out of the corner of his eye that Bridger again had his back to him. The MD was now sitting motionless - facing the brick wall in front of him. Don't turn around please, thought Mackay, as he saw the familiar Blake and Lander fax header begin to appear from the depths of the fax machine. The fax read as follows:

Avon and General Insurance
23-27 Bernard Street
BRISTOL
BS8 6NE
Tel. 0117 909 6000
Fax. 0117 909 6001

Mr Jonathan Bridger
Managing Director
Everyman Credit Ltd
No 2 Connaught Lane
Victoria
LONDON
SW1 7RQ

15 March 1992

Dear Jonathan

Everyman Credit Ltd
Master Credit Insurance – Policy No. CF/89/762
Profit Share Payment

Further to our telephone conversation of yesterday, I am pleased to confirm that the profit share payable to Everyman Credit Ltd. under the terms of Policy CF/89/762 is £7,016,232.67. Further to your instructions, I also confirm that the above sum has been remitted to the Gibraltar and West Mediterranean Bank, account no. 763821.

Can I take this opportunity to thank you again for your business.

I do hope that there will be fresh opportunities which we can again develop jointly in the future.

Yours sincerely

James Millard

JAMES MILLARD
Director

Bloody Hell, thought Mackay, reading it again. This is serious. Where had the rest of the seven million gone? Was it still in account no.763821? Was Bridger acting alone? Surely each account would require two signatures. Was Platt's death just a coincidence? Who had archived those boxes?

He quickly photocopied the document and wrote in the corner of the photocopy, 'to be given to Detective Inspector Steele (c/o New Scotland Yard) if anything unusual should happen to me.' He then dated it and put it in an envelope addressed to himself care of his parent's house. On his way to Bridger's office he popped the letter into Everyman's outgoing mail.

Without saying a word, Mackay sat down opposite Bridger and handed him the letter. The banker flexed the letter between his thumb and forefinger several times before starting to read it. When he'd finished, he handed it back to Mackay, and looked directly at him.

'It's a mistake,' said Bridger aggressively. 'I know of no such rebate.'

'Has Everyman ever had an insurance policy with Avon and General?' said Mackay evenly.

'Not to my knowledge,' replied Bridger.

'I have further correspondence addressed to you from Avon and General back in 1990,' continued Mackay, 'why is that do you think?'

'Maybe the roof sprang a leak and we made a claim,' said Bridger flippantly. Mackay felt out of his depth. Perhaps this had been a cock up by Avon and General after all, and he was simply wasting his client's time.

'OK, I'm sorry to have wasted your time with this, but I feel I should pass it on to Inspector Steele, as it could be vital to his investigation.' Mackay was pleased to see Bridger shift uneasily in his chair after this comment. So not an error by Avon and General after all, he thought.

'Don't you think you should consult your boss before informing the police? If that letter is genuine, and I'm not saying that it is, it means that you and your colleagues have missed quite a large fraud. This is after all only a small company, where can seven million simply have vanished to?'

'You tell me Jonathan, you're the Managing Director.'

'Let's just for the sake of argument say that the whole seven million - plus interest - had, as of today, all been completely repaid. Let's say that the money had simply been misplaced and had never gone missing. What may have happened for example is that a foolish individual, an ageing banker perhaps, had piled into property - in the late 80s and early 90s - and got stung. Perhaps that banker had needed several hundred thousand pounds to keep him liquid - only until the property market had recovered of course, which it now has.'

'Why would this ageing banker need seven million then?' probed Mackay.

'Far easier to hide no rebate than part of a rebate,' said Bridger.

'Until this year that is. How did Platt pick this up?'

'No idea, he should have been a copper that one.'

'Did he challenge you on it?'

'Yep, I just passed it onto Silas and he discussed it with him.' There was a pause as each man took stock of the situation. So Craven knew. It was Mackay who continued first.

'And the hit and run, Platt's death I mean, purely a coincidence right?' Bridger's jaw dropped at this, he looked shaken.

'You don't surely think that I'd anything to do with that do you? Who do you think I am?' His denial was robust enough to seem genuine, and Mackay believed him. There was a silence as each man pondered what would happen next.

'What will you do now?' said Bridger, speaking his mind. 'Whistleblowers never come out of these situations winners you know. If you go to the Police, your own firm and my bank will sue you for breach of confidentiality. On the other hand...' He paused, and let the words hang in the air for a moment. '...I'm sure the three of us can come to some sort of arrangement. After all, nothing's been actually stolen has it?'

'You're lucky the property market's bounced back, otherwise a cover up wouldn't be an option.'

'Quite,' said Bridger. There was another pause as Mackay fiddled with the Avon and General letter and Bridger flicked his Biro on and off repeatedly.

'So Silas knows about this,' said Mackay. 'Has he benefited?'

'Not to my knowledge,' replied Bridger, 'he's just helping out an old chum.'

'That's not like him, is this anything to do with Gibraltar?' Mackay saw that he'd connected with this one. Bridger's head had recoiled three inches as soon as the words had left Mackay's lips.

'Er... Gibraltar,' floundered Bridger, 'how do you know about that?'

'A journalist friend of mine has been digging around and come up with some scandal that he was involved in during the 70s. Know anything about that?'

'Er...no...' said the banker unconvincingly, 'if you've got any questions on Gibraltar you'd better ask Silas himself. I know very little about what went on then.' Bridger stopped flicking his pen and put it into his jacket pocket. He saw Inspector Steele come out of the door by the lift. 'Listen, you'd better decide what you want to do quickly,' he said urgently. 'I've got an appointment with Inspector Plod now.' Mackay turned in his chair and saw the policeman heading towards them.

'Give me your home number, I'll call you tonight.' Bridger brought a business card out of his desk drawer and scribbled a number on the back of it. Mackay picked it up and put it in his wallet as the policeman knocked at the door.

'Come in Inspector,' said Bridger, 'we are just finishing...'

'Anything unusual cropped up yet Mr Mackay?' asked the policeman.

'No, just the normal number crunching,' replied Mackay credibly. He looked at Bridger, then left.

CHAPTER 13

(TUESDAY 29TH APRIL 1997 - THE SAME DAY)

The phone rang, even before Steadman had had a chance to finish his Benjy's coffee.

'Mr Steadman?'

'Yes.'

'It's Anne Gill here, we met last Friday.'

'How are you Anne, did you have a good weekend?'

'Yes, thank you. Look, I'll come straight to the point. I think you should come back up here. Your visit got me thinking and I've been rummaging about the Hall all weekend trying to find Penny's journal. I've found it, and I think you should read it.'

'Can't you post it down to me,' said Steadman, already thinking about his bloated expense claim. 'I promise I'll look after it.'

'No. I'm not comfortable doing that Nick, it's not mine, and I doubt if I'm supposed to have it. Besides, there's somebody else up here who'd also like to talk to you about Silas Craven. Old Joe thinks he's remembered something.'

'Ok Anne, sounds interesting. I'll just clear it with my boss and head up. If I can get away soon, I should be with you late afternoon.' With that he put down the phone and headed into Metcalfe's office. The office was empty so he turned towards the door but a rustling of paper from behind Metcalfe's desk halted him.

'Hello,' he said apprehensively.

'Is that you Nick?' came the editor's reply. 'I'm over here, my back's gone again.'

'Golf or squash this time?' said Steadman, peering over the desk at the horizontal Metcalfe.

'Golf. The sweetest four iron I've hit for a while. Worth every second of pain.'

'Any objection if I head north again? I've just had a call from that old woman I told you about on the phone, says she's found a journal which will dish the dirt on Craven.'

'When are you thinking of going?'

'Well, I'll have to go now if we want anything for Thursday.'

'Anything from that bean-counter who went to Gibraltar?'

'No, I haven't spoken to him yet.'

'Ok, you whiz up, but try and get the last train back to avoid a hotel bill.' The editor tried to turn onto his side but instead grimaced and gave up.

Steadman returned to his desk and saw that there'd been a phone message from Mackay. He called the number which was written on the post-it but there was no reply. He then flicked through his recently acquired GNER timetable and noted that there was a train leaving at 11.50.

This time his run to King's Cross was quick and uneventful, and he was soon on the train which set off punctually. Unlike the previous Thursday, it was on time all of the way and he arrived at Alnmouth at 3.30. He was the only passenger who got off and he was greeted by the same grey whiskered station master with the green flag. It was clear that the station master had a poor memory for faces when he asked, 'come far sir?'

'London,' replied Steadman.

'Thought so, you look like you need a bit of a holiday,' was the stock reply.

'OK, I'll take it easy then. Does the train always run on time when it's in BR's old livery?' said Steadman mischievously.

'Always,' said the station master. 'I'm still waiting for the private sector benefits to filter through. As long as they don't muck about with my pension I don't care - I've only got three years to go.'

'Maybe Labour will renationalise it on Friday morning,' said Steadman.

'Maybe,' said the man, distracted by the southbound 15.35 which rounded the bend.

Given the sexual extras which might be available at the Schooner Hotel that night, Steadman had absolutely no intention of catching the last London bound train, so the first thing he did was check in. He was disappointed that the reception desk was manned by the cheeky young barman cum waiter instead of Judith.

'It's Judith's day off,' he said slyly, before Steadman had had a chance to ask where she was. 'She'll be in later though, she always has her nights off in the bar anyway.'

'Thanks,' said Steadman, caught between picking up the room key and clipping the lad behind the ear. He took the key option and dropped his overnight bag in his room, then headed off towards Keepers Cottage. His route took him past the Dower House and as he drew level with the building he saw Craven's mother sitting in the large bay window drinking tea. She saw him instantly and gave him a frosty look before picking up the phone and dialling. Although he couldn't hear anything, he was sure she was calling her son.

Whilst Spring had arrived in the capital, Winter was having a last kick in the north east and the air brought on shore from the North Sea by the strong easterly wind was very cold. The temperature contrast between the exterior and interior of Keepers Cottage couldn't have been more marked and Steadman was soon wrapped in the comfortable old armchair, tea in one hand, dribbly scone in the other.

'Now Nick,' said Anne Gill, her green eyes infusing him with her life force, 'there it is, finish your scone first, I don't want you to drop butter on it.' Steadman stuffed the remainder of the scone into his mouth and began to read the large leather bound journal.

The early years were the stuff of ordinary little rich girls, of horses, grand houses, hunting, shooting, fishing and glittering balls held in draughty castles. The journal described the early death of her mother and her father's appointment of a housekeeper shortly afterwards. The housekeeper's husband,

Alan Craven, had been killed in a mining accident the previous year. So the offer of employment, whilst genuine, had also had charitable motives. Mrs Craven's son, Silas - as the years went by - gradually became one of the family.

Whilst Penny's brother David enjoyed the physical side of farming he had no aptitude for the Estate's administration, whereas Silas was gifted with numbers and a good organiser. Indeed so successful was he at managing the Estate that it showed a small profit for the first time in nearly fifty years. It was only natural that David began to feel threatened and his relationship with Craven began to deteriorate. Things got much worse during the spring of 1963 when Silas and Penny returned from Gretna Green married. David and Silas's differences became irreconcilable, so Basil was forced to offer them an estate cottage and secure Silas a position at Parker and Co, the local accountant. It was here, 31 December 1963, that the journal ended.

'Very interesting,' began Steadman, 'but to be honest not a great deal of journalistic value here Anne.'

'But where's the rest of it?' replied the virtual nonagenarian rhetorically. 'Where's 1964? Where's the last seven months of her life? I've looked all over the Hall but I can't find it anywhere. She must've hidden it to keep it away from Craven. Joe thinks he knows where it might be. He'll meet you in the Schooner at 8.00.'

'OK,' said Steadman, stumbling forward as the armchair springs propelled him forcefully. 'I'll let you know if I find anything out.' When he opened the door to leave, the wind blew in with such ferocity that several lace doilies took off and Mrs Gill's husband made one last flight across the room - almost shattering the glass in his photo frame as he crash landed onto the floor.

'Stay away from the cliff path in this wind,' she warned, and then closed the door.

The short walk back to the hotel took longer than usual as Steadman was forced to lean into the wind all the way. Even with the heavy oak door to the Schooner firmly closed, the wind still whistled through the bar, lifting the browning pennants and rattling the rusted anchors. There was no sign of Judith or Joe, so Steadman tried to avoid conversation with the cheeky young barman whilst he pulled his pint.

'Maybe Jude's not coming in tonight,' said the youth with feigned innocence.

'Right,' said Steadman, trying to sound disinterested, but feeling foolish as a beer mat stubbornly refused to disengage itself from the bottom of his pint glass. Before he'd had a chance to pay, he caught a glimpse of a blue peaked cap of the Uncle Albert style out of the corner of his eye.

'I'll have a Federation please son,' said the blue peaked cap. They sat in the same wooden booth they'd sat in the previous week. Joe had drunk half of his pint before he spoke again. 'Of course when I talked to you the other day I didn't think to tell you I'd seen Penny Gray the night that she died. It was a night much the same as this, a gale force wind, but warmer. I was up at the castle watching the boats hurry in when she scurried by. I didn't really notice at the time, but meeting you last week and talking to old Anne Gill reminded me that she was carrying some sort of book. I never thought to mention it back then given that the police were so certain it was an accident - but now I'm not so sure. What happened to that book? There was no sign of it when they found the body.'

'Perhaps she hid it in the castle Joe,' said Steadman. He paused. 'Why were the police so sure that it was an accident?'

'No motive for anything else. As far as the village was concerned she and Craven had the perfect marriage - and she didn't hide it in the castle, I would have seen.'

'What's further along the path?'

'Nothing really until you get to Craster - just a few World War Two bunkers.' He paused again. 'She could have hidden it in one of those. I remember her and her brother used to play in the nearest one when they were kids.'

'How far past the castle?' said the journalist, rising to his feet.

'Leave it til the morning,' said Joe, looking alarmed, 'it'll be dark soon and the path will be treacherous in this wind.'

'Don't worry about me Joe - I was in the Boy Scouts you know.'

Steadman began to regret his decision even before he'd left the bar. It took him three huge heaves to open the heavy oak door - which was effectively locked by the strength of the wind - and once in the street, the wind tried to blow him into the path of an oncoming bus which only missed him by a whisker.

The path up to the castle was more sheltered but the noise was incredible. The intense howling of the wind was interrupted at regular intervals by a deafening thud from the block-hole, which sent huge plumes of sea-water crashing over the walls and onto the path. Steadman was soon wet with spray as he half stumbled and half slipped down the path at the far side of the castle. He saw that the tide was out. This was fortunate as it meant he could cut across the pebbly beach onto the next headland. Even in the half light he could see a concrete pill box silhouetted against the skyline in front of him. Joe had told him that there'd been a scare in 1940 that Hitler might come from Norway, so hundreds of these pill boxes had been built, more as observation posts than as serious defensive structures.

The rear part of the pillbox had been dug into the side of the bank and it took Steadman several minutes to find the narrow trench which led to an even narrower door which was sunk low into the concrete. He crawled in on his hands and knees. It was dark inside and it reeked of urine. He flicked on his cigarette lighter and saw instantly that he was at the right place, as the initials 'DG' and 'PG' had been carved into the concrete with the date '17 March 1956.'

He sensed at once that the missing diary was buried under the pile of stones in the corner of the pillbox, and after a couple of minutes of scratching around he found it, wrapped in a greasy canvas bag and tied up with twine. It was difficult holding his cigarette lighter and taking notes as he read, but there was still some light coming from the slit at the front of the pillbox and he was completely sheltered from the wind. By the time the flame flickered and died with the last of the lighter fluid, he had jotted down most of what he needed.

He peered out of the machine gun slit and saw that there was very little light left. The sea was a mass of white splashes as the wind continually whipped up the surf - no way the Wehrmacht would have been coming tonight thought Steadman, as he turned to crawl out of the pillbox. He stood and looked towards the castle, which in the semi-darkness appeared to bar his way home, and he saw a torch flicker from within the gatehouse. Another idiot out on a night like this he thought, as he slid down the path onto the pebbly beach.

By the time he had crossed the bay and started to climb towards the castle it was so dark that he could barely see the path. The lights from the village pointed to the general direction, but the path seemed intent on traversing every slippery rock and deep ditch in the county. The wind howling through the ramparts was incessant and the continuous thud from the block-hole sounded like a barrage. He made his way cautiously through the compound until the path narrowed once again between the wall and the cliff edge. Even in the daylight, it was doubtful whether Steadman would have seen the stocky man who cowered in the gatehouse. So when he half turned to face the man, after his note book and journal had been snatched, he was caught off balance and the wind blew him over the edge onto Greymare Rocks.

CHAPTER 14

(TUESDAY 29TH APRIL 1997 - THE SAME DAY)

As soon as he'd finished parrying Inspector Steele's ineffectual and widely inaccurate questioning, Bridger picked up his briefcase and headed out of his office. 'I'll finish this report at home, June,' he said unconvincingly, as he passed his secretary on his way out of the building.

Once outside he turned left and walked behind the Army and Navy Stores. He skirted by Westminster Cathedral and soon arrived at the Edwardian Mansion block that served as his weekday home.

The one bedroom fifth floor flat was sparsely decorated and reflected its status as a place to sleep rather than a home. He looked at the pictures of his wife and children that sat on the top shelf of the alcove cupboard next to the gas fire. He then took off his jacket, kicked off his shoes and poured himself a very large Highland Park from the already open bottle.

Mackay's questioning had unsettled him. It had never occurred to the banker that Platt's death might not have been an accident and could be linked to the insurance rebate. If it was murder, then there could only be one suspect, but Silas had been with him the Friday night that Platt had died. Was Silas up to hiring a contract killer? The thought was preposterous, but Bridger knew that Craven could be ruthless. He thought back to the Gibraltar and Atlantic General Trading Company scandal and Peter Vassallo's death.

He had arrived in Gibraltar newly promoted as the manager of the bank's branch. The position was the first he'd had with any real responsibility - and in those days branch managers did have real responsibility. As well as finding new business he was tasked with approving new credit lines. So towards the end of his first year in charge - when he was just short of his annual target - Peter Vassallo had walked in with the rosiest business plan that Bridger had ever seen. It was a licence to print money.

At that time every single item that was sold in Gibraltar came in by air or sea. So when Franco died, and the prospect of cheap goods flooding in by land became a reality, Bridger was convinced that the bank should jump onto the band wagon along with everybody else. His quick appraisal of Vassallo's trading history revealed solid year on year growth, the accounts were audited and signed off by Blake and Scott, and Vassallo himself was plausible and trustworthy, a brilliant businessman. As the requested £50,000 was within his authority limits, Bridger approved the loan and remitted the funds himself.

About a month later, he'd seen Vassallo at a New Year's Eve reception given by the Governor at the Convent. Vassallo was in the corner of the room gesticulating wildly at another man, who stood motionless, absorbing the Gibraltan's malevolence. As Bridger approached them they abruptly broke off their conversation and turned to greet him. Vassallo was now all sweetness and light. The other man remained expressionless.

'Ah, my good friend Jonathan Bridger,' said Vassallo. 'Allow me to introduce you to my accountant, Silas Craven.'

'Nice to meet you,' said Craven, taking the banker's hand. 'I understand Peter is our mutual client.'

'Yes,' said Bridger evenly. He had been a little disconcerted at Vassallo's intemperate behaviour and more than concerned that the conversation had ended so abruptly as he'd approached. He looked more closely at Craven and saw a man with film star looks, more elegant than Clark Gable yet no Cary Grant, a mix. There was an uncomfortable silence. Bridger looked at his shoes and was glad when the large group of acolytes surrounding the Governor roared into laughter, giving him the opportunity to look at something other than his feet. When the laughter died down there was a second silence. It was Craven who spoke first, and as he spoke he smiled so warmly at Bridger that the words which left his lips - words which Bridger had been half expecting - seemed to be coated with sugar.

'There may be a problem with your loan,' said the accountant, letting the full impact of every banker's nightmare sink in.

'Oh,' said Bridger weakly.

'The thing is,' continued Craven, 'the border isn't going to be opened this year and Peter's got a lot of rotting stock in his warehouses. I'm afraid most of it will have to be written off.'

'How much is left of the fifty?' said Bridger.

'Not much,' replied Vassallo, 'most of it's been used to pay off the trade creditors. I'll struggle to meet January's wage bill.'

'Christ,' said the wretched banker slowly, 'you've really stitched me up.' Bridger knew that it was a career ending error, and he lashed out at the two closest targets. 'I won't go down alone for this,' he snapped.

Craven took a step towards him and put his hand on his arm and held it tightly. The accountant looked the banker directly in the eye and gave him one of his syrupy smiles. Bridger looked away unable to hold his stare.

'There's no need to do anything hasty,' said Craven comfortingly, 'there'll be a solution to this problem.'

The solution, of course, was to throw more money at the Gibraltar and Atlantic General Trading Company. As the documentation for the original £50,000 loan was still on Bridger's desk, it was easy to issue a new loan agreement which showed a £75,000 loan payable in two tranches. Bridger remitted the second tranche of £25,000 shortly before the end of January at the same time as Craven certified the Company's accounts. Bridger never had discovered why Craven had been so helpful to Vassallo. Sure, the banker had relied on Blake and Scott's opinion when he'd advanced the original loan, but Craven could have wriggled out of that. He was sure that

Vassallo had some other hold over him.

Things went smoothly for the next few months. Before Vassallo's gamble on the border crossing had gone wrong, his company had traded reasonably well. So he was able to service the debt and Bridger even began to think that given time, some capital repayments might be possible. Those hopes were dashed in September of that year when Vassallo and Craven came into his office. It was a hot day and Bridger could see that Vassallo was sweating profusely through his open necked shirt. The grocer looked haggard but excitable. He opened his briefcase and slapped an all too familiar business plan onto Bridger's desk. Without hesitating the banker pushed the document back to Vassallo.

'No way,' said Bridger, 'no more money.'

'But Jonathan,' began Vassallo, 'we are such good friends. We need each other. The border will open this time. I will repay all of your money. We will all be rich.'

'No,' said Bridger forcefully. 'Even if I wanted to, a fresh loan so soon would raise eyebrows at Head Office.' He looked at Craven for support but there was none forthcoming, instead Vassallo continued.

'But I've been so good to you these last few months Jonathan, we've had a lot of fun have we not?' Vassallo's meaning was clear. Whilst Bridger hadn't taken a bribe as such, there had of course been perks. He had eaten in the best restaurants this side of Paris, paid for nothing, and enjoyed (on a temporary basis) the company of one beautiful woman after another.

'Are you threatening me Peter?' asked Bridger calmly.

'Not at all Jonathan. I'm merely pointing out that the three of us have formed a close bond.' He paused to choose his words carefully. 'It would be difficult to see how we could survive as individuals if those bonds were …er… fractured.'

There was silence. Vassallo pushed the business plan back to Bridger.

Craven, who had sat expressionless up to this point, interjected. 'Let's not be hasty now, why don't we let Jonathan have a think about our proposal and revisit the subject tomorrow, over dinner at the Mons Calpe.'

The grocer and the banker nodded their heads in agreement and all three men got up to shake hands. Bridger looked at Vassallo, then at Craven.

Craven tipped his head slightly as he took Bridger's hand, purring 'don't worry about it Jonathan, I'll sort this out.'

Bridger got up from his seat and poured himself another large Highland Park. There was a draught coming through the kitchen door which was ajar, so he closed it and turned up the gas fire to maximum before settling down again in his armchair.

When Craven had said, 'I'll sort this out,' it *had* crossed Bridger's mind at the time that Vassallo's death had been remarkably convenient. Sure, by the time Vassallo had entered the Mons Calpe he was very drunk and it had always seemed more likely to Bridger that he'd stumbled and fallen rather than jumped off himself. But now he wasn't so sure. It later transpired that Vassallo and Craven had been drinking all day but Craven had appeared sober to Bridger. As soon as they'd arrived at the restaurant the subject of the loan was brought up and the conversation had quickly become heated - but without the professional restraint of the previous day. Vassallo had in turns become aggressive, then conciliatory, then morose, but never suicidal. Craven had looked on impassively as the Gibraltan had delivered his drunken diatribe against the Spanish, bankers and then the British.

When Vassallo had got up for a piss and Craven had followed him out shortly afterwards for a cigar, it had never occurred to Bridger that Craven had had anything to do with Vassallo's permanent failure to return. The subsequent investigation had indeed been lightweight. And hinted at the authorities' desire to quickly suppress any financial scandal which might suggest that the colony couldn't regulate itself. Could Craven have pushed Vassallo off the top of the Rock, calmly walked back to the table, poured himself another brandy, then courteously asked after the health of Bridger's family? It seemed incredible.

Bridger's recollections were abruptly interrupted by the buzzer to the external door. He got up and walked to the internal phone and picked it up.

CHAPTER 15

(WEDNESDAY 30TH APRIL 1997)

HESELTINE WARNS NATION SLEEPWALKING TO DISASTER
MAJOR SAYS 'NEW LABOUR' IS A 'GREAT MARKETING SCAM'
MOBUTU TO MEET REBEL LEADER ON SOUTH AFRICAN SHIP

Mackay had slept fitfully and doubted whether he'd had much REM. He had tried to call Bridger several times during the evening but there had been no reply. All night he had wondered what he was going to do. The money had been repaid, the seven million could still be included in this year's figures, he himself would likely benefit if he kept quiet, everyone was a winner. Was there really any harm done? The consequences of opening his mouth were dreadful. He would be sacked and sued by both Blakes and Everyman for breaches of confidentiality, Bridger and possibly Craven would go to prison and the Tory party would absorb yet another scandal.

He got out of bed and decided that before doing anything else he would confront Craven with what he knew. This would serve the dual purpose of hearing Craven's side of it and finding out what was in it for him if he kept quiet. He knew the Tories had had it anyway and he didn't give a shit about Craven. Bridger he liked, but he was more concerned about his own welfare. Who would employ him without references? Nobody liked a whistleblower.

He showered and dressed quickly then breezed through the kitchen without stopping for breakfast. It was unusual for him to be up before Atif and Ed, but even more unusual for him to catch the 7.50, where he quickly found that the earlier hour made quite a difference, and he struggled to get on.

Instead of the usual calm hush punctuated by the occasional tense conversation, the carriage was completely silent, as each commuter no doubt wondered what impact, on them, the new Government would have. Mackay glanced around the carriage and saw the usual mix of men in grey suits, young City workers and graduate trainees. Were, after eighteen years, the good times coming to an end? New Labour had no friends on this train, thought Mackay, as he saw the platform approach and he felt the train slow to a walking pace. The silence and glum faces of Mackay's fellow passengers evoked comparisons with the French Revolution. Was the carriage a tumbril carrying the Ancien Regime to the Place de la Westminster where Madame la Blair waited, patiently, with a sharp tax hike?

It was the first time that year that Mackay had beaten Tony King into the office. When the diminutive auditor arrived to see Mackay at his desk - already working - it upset his value system, so much so that despite opening his mouth to say something, no words came out. Mackay ignored him and flicked through the internal phone directory. He found Craven's number and dialled. He wasn't surprised that there was no answer. He'll be in the constituency shaking hands and kissing babies by now, thought Mackay.

To make sure, Mackay took the lift up to the sixth floor and again found Craven's office, which was empty. As there was a Burberry overcoat and a black umbrella in the room, and as Craven's briefcase lay semi-ajar on the large mahogany desk, it was clear that Craven was putting to the test what the 'safe' in 'safe seat' actually meant. Mackay took a pen out of his pocket and walked over to the desk, intending to leave Craven a post-it note asking him to call him when he returned to his office. As Mackay bent down he glanced into the briefcase and saw a large, green, hard backed A4 notebook. In the top right hand corner, inscribed in silver, were the words 'Borough Gazette.' What the fuck's Craven doing with that, thought Mackay?

Then a noise from the corridor prompted him to begin writing. He heard somebody come into the room behind him and he turned to face Craven.

'What are you up to Tom?' said the partner evenly.

'Just leaving you a note,' replied Mackay, a little too quickly.

'About what?'

'Everyman.'

Craven walked past Mackay and sat down at his desk with his back to him. He gently closed his briefcase and pointed to the seat next to him, indicating that he should sit down. Mackay did as he was instructed and sat at right angles to his boss. Without looking at him, Craven continued.

'What about Everyman?' There was a lengthy pause. 'You know how busy I am at the moment.'

'I've found a seven million pound insurance rebate that went missing for about five years.'

Mackay looked for some sort of reaction from Craven, but there wasn't one, instead he sat impassively looking out of the window. Mackay's words continued to linger until the phone rang. As the ringing persisted, and as it was clear that Craven wasn't going to answer, Mackay reached forward to pick it up.

'Leave it,' snapped Craven, with such ferocity that Mackay flinched back into his chair. They sat in silence and when the ringing eventually stopped, Craven slowly spun round in his chair to face Mackay full on. There was a black, icy, savage quality to his eyes, which unsettled Mackay and evaporated his earlier boldness. It was Craven who continued, 'seven million you say?'

'Yes.'

'Has Bridger confirmed this to you?'

'More or less, and besides, I have third party evidence.'

'Third party evidence?'

'Yes'. Mackay hesitated before continuing. 'He said that you knew about it, he said Keith Platt had told you.'

'That's a lie,' said Craven softly.

It was obvious that he'd regained his composure, so Mackay, with a daring usually alien to him determined to see if he could rattle Craven again. 'Did you work with Bridger in the 70s?' There was no reply, so Mackay continued. 'Have you ever been to Gibraltar, Silas?'

Craven gave Mackay his warm treacly smile and drew him in. He was back in control, confident, assured and unflappable. 'What of it, Tom?' he said innocently.

'Well ...I ... he...' blurted Mackay, 'Bridger, I mean.' Mackay stopped to gather his thoughts and order the words in his mind. Craven continued to eyeball him. His unremitting stare penetrated Mackay and seemed to disconnect his brain. Had they been on a street corner in Brixton 'What you looking at?' would have been the appropriate response. Instead Mackay stumbled on, his attempt to rattle Craven melting away. 'The thing is Silas, Bridger hinted that there may have been some sort of scandal.'

Craven got up from his seat signifying that the meeting was over. As Mackay stood up, Craven put one hand on his shoulder and took his arm with the other. 'The delusions of a has-been banker Tom. Don't you worry about this rebate or talk of scandal, I'll sort it out. Group have had their suspicions about Bridger for a while now. These sort of accusations aren't helpful.' He paused. 'Will I see you at the constituency tonight?'

'Er, maybe Silas,' replied Mackay, bewildered by the sudden switch to normality. 'I've one or two things to do at home first.'

'Be great if you could make it,' said Craven, further extending his smile to the full yard, 'I do value your support.' With that, he closed the door and Mackay was out in the corridor.

As the lift descended into the bowels of the building, Mackay pondered on Craven's parting remarks. Had there been a hidden meaning there? If there had, did Craven think Mackay came that cheaply? The delusions of a has-been banker Craven had said - yet Bridger had told Mackay that Craven had known about the rebate. It seemed more likely that a desperate Bridger had threatened to lift the lid on the Gibraltar scandal, and that to keep him quiet, Craven had ignored the temporary disappearance of the seven million.

He arrived back at his own office to find the nubile Sally Purcell deep in conversation with Tony King. As he entered the room they broke off their conversation and she sat down on his desk. King acknowledged Mackay with a slight nod of the head and set off in the direction of the coffee machine.

'What were you talking to Wan about?' said Mackay nonchalantly.

'I told him we were an item.'

'What did he think of that?'

'Fairly shocked. He thinks I should still be in mourning and draped from head to foot in black. Besides, I think he was a bit jealous. He fancies me.'

'Christ, is there anybody in this Department who doesn't?' Mackay turned to look at her and she smiled at him tenderly. God she was attractive. He glanced at the semi-open door and was tempted to close it, lock it, and jump on her then and there. 'Talking of your admirers, I've got a little job for you.'

'What?'

'I want you to lure Craven out of his office for twenty minutes so that I can pinch something out of his briefcase.'

'Not more conspiracy theories,' she said.

'Not a theory my dear, hard evidence. Craven's got that journalist's notebook.' She shifted nervously on the desk, realising that Mackay was serious. Here was a real test of her commitment to him. 'Are you doing any work for him at the moment?' continued Mackay.

'Just a shitty Unit Trust, I'll need something more to get him to come down here.'

'You'll have to play the sexual card then.'

'No, he'd guess that something was up, I gave him quite a knock back when he made a pass at me before.' She paused to think. 'He smokes. I'll tell him Keith told me something about the Everyman job and he can meet me outside for a fag.'

'Brilliant. But you'd better do it quickly. I don't want him scooting off briefcase and all.' With a seated semi-twirl worthy of Anthea Redfern she reached out for the phone and picked it up. He saw her dial 0 for the internal switchboard and purse her lips.

'Silas Craven please.' She flicked her hair as she waited to be connected. 'Silas, it's Sally Purcell.' He saw her shift her weight to her left buttock as she listened to the condolences streaming eloquently from the sixth floor. As the flow subsided, she flicked her hair again and again pursed her lips. 'Silas, I really am fine thank you.' She paused. 'The reason why I'm calling is something Keith said to me, it's been troubling me. I think it might be important.'

There was silence.

Mackay wished he was a fly on the wall in Craven's office, observing his reaction. Instead he watched as Sally flicked her hair for the third time and re-purse her pursed lips.

'I'd rather not talk about it in the building,' she continued, 'will you meet me at the St Michael's Street exit for a smoke?'

There was a short pause and she put the phone down. Craven had agreed. 'What shall I tell him?' she said, performing the reverse seated semi-twirl to bring her directly in front of him on the desk.

'Just that Keith mentioned that the seven million was bothering him, and that he was going to mention it to Craven. You're just making sure that that conversation took place.'

'What if he tries to push me under a cab?'

'Just turn and face it and it'll bounce off,' replied Mackay, with a dirty smile.

'For God's sake be serious, Tom, I don't like this. You and your conspiracy theories, you should have worked for MI5.'

'What conspiracy theories are those then?' said Tony King, walking back into the room, coffee in hand.

'Well thanks for getting us coffees Tony,' said Sally sweetly, giving him her seductive half-smile.

'Er, well, sorry Sal…, what do you want?' He put his coffee

on the desk and started back towards the door.
'Only joking Mr King,' she said, deliberately brushing past him on her way out, 'I'm off on an errand.'
'Me too,' echoed Mackay, and Tony King was left standing motionless, inhaling her scent.
Mackay headed for the sandwich bar on the fourth floor which was the only part of the building which overlooked the St Michael's Street 'smokers' area.' The sandwich bar had always been there and looked very much as it did when Mackay had joined the firm six years ago - despite being 'enhanced' when the staff restaurant had been closed the previous year. It was too early for lunch traffic, but there was the usual collection of has-beens from the Personnel Department who were buying the 'real' cappuccinos which were hardly better than the muck which was dispensed from the machines.
Mackay propped himself against the floor to ceiling window at the far end of the room and looked out over St Michael's Street. There was no sign of Sally yet amongst the dozen or so shirt sleeved smokers who fidgeted uncomfortably between gasps. But then he saw her come out of the building and stand off one of the smaller groups of greying men who were partially secreted in the doorway of the fire exit. None of the men acknowledged her, but Mackay chuckled as he saw one of them subconsciously run his hand through his hair and another move his feet to stand fully astride a manhole cover - they were aware of her presence. Mackay could see that the tallest of the three men who was closest to her was toying with the idea of offering her a light. Then Mackay saw him fumble in his jacket pocket - how many relationships have started like this he thought - but the man's hand reappeared without his lighter as Craven emerged from nowhere and stood aggressively between Sally and the group of would-be suitors. Mackay caught a glimpse of her giving Craven her much practiced helpless look, as he turned from the window to head for the stairs.
He ran up them two at a time and he was soon in the corridor leading to Craven's office. As he approached, he saw Craven's

secretary Sarah at the far end of the corridor walking towards him. She would reach the office first. God, I hope she's not going in thought Mackay, as Sarah caught his eye about twenty feet in front of him and smiled as she turned left into Craven's office. Mackay glanced through the door as he drew level with Craven's room and then walked towards the stairs at the other end of the building. A notice board gave him the opportunity of legitimately loitering. He stood and wondered how long it would take Sarah to finish the note he'd seen her writing on Craven's desk.

Mackay had observed Sarah's masculine appearance when he'd first met her the previous week, but she had been pleasant enough and his attitude to her since then had not been hostile. Now, however, every passing minute that he stood at the notice board accentuated her ugliness. Her fuzzy top lip became a grotesque moustache and her occasional acne was converted to a widespread pox. He read the firm's insurance policy document for the sixth time. What the hell was she doing in there?

Eventually, out of the corner of his eye, he saw her leave the office and shuffle back to her own room. He turned and walked calmly back along the corridor and into Craven's office. The briefcase was where it had been earlier and it was closed. Despite his shaking hands, it opened without a problem and he quickly found the green hard backed notebook with the letters NJS written under the Borough Gazette. He hastily closed the briefcase and rapidly retraced his steps to the fourth floor sandwich bar. He resumed his earlier position and again looked out of the floor to ceiling window. Sally was talking to the tall man who had reached for his lighter earlier but Craven was gone. Mackay shifted a few feet to his right so that he was in full view from the street below. Sally saw him instantly. He gave her the thumbs up and she feigned wiping sweat from her brow. He saw her say something to the tall man, drop her cigarette on the pavement, stub it out with her shoe, then turn and go back into the building. He saw the tall man say something to his mates and they all laughed. He met her in his empty office a few minutes later and he saw that her face was flushed with excitement. It suited her. 'Well, what did he say?'

'I could see he was interested,' she said, 'though he did say that Keith had mentioned something about it, which weakens your conspiracy theory a bit.'

'That's not what he told me, he's probably trying to distance himself from Bridger.' Mackay fingered the journal whilst wondering what to do next. 'Look, why don't we knock off at 5 and head back to mine to read this book properly. I'll try the Borough Gazette again to see if they've heard from their boy. Let's keep our heads down until then.'

'Fine,' she replied, heading out of the room. 'Let's audit.'

The rest of the day was largely uneventful. Mackay was put straight through to the editor of the Gazette when he tried to get hold of Steadman. And he detected a note of concern in Metcalfe's voice when he told Mackay that he was uncertain of Steadman's whereabouts.

'Have you been helping him out with his election coverage?' asked the editor.

'Something like that,' replied Mackay, glancing furtively at the spine of Steadman's notebook which was just visible in his briefcase.

'If he tries to contact you, do me a favour and let me know. 'It's unlike him to go AWOL.'

'Of course.'

At 5 pm, Mackay picked Sally up from her office and together they walked to Waterloo to catch a train to Wandsworth. They just missed the 5.20 so Mackay decided to use Route B and go to Clapham Junction and walk from there.

The walk from Clapham Junction took longer than usual because they had to skirt around a mob of aggressive Labour supporters who had surrounded a small contingent of Tory activists. The outnumbered Conservatives had flung a thin piquet line around their MP, but the line had been breached in several places - allowing the left wing yobs to pelt the besieged Parliamentarian with rotten eggs.

'Aren't you going to help?' asked Sally, as they avoided a fearsome looking leather jacket-clad socialist who lurched towards them in a Yosser Hughes like manner.

'Not in my constituency,' replied Mackay, 'we must be in Battersea here.'

They reached the flat without further incident. Mackay knew that Ed was on a course and there was no sign of Atif. The flat was empty. Since Mackay's suggestion that they examine the notebook in bed was flatly refused they sat down at the kitchen table and leafed through Steadman's unwieldy scribble.

'Despite knowing a little short-hand I'm struggling to decipher this, Tom,' said Sally after about an hour. 'There's nothing in the long-hand to suggest anything untoward either - I'm beginning to half-believe Craven's side of it. What really surprises me is that he's a Geordie. I must say he's hidden his humble origins very well.'

'Mmm...' mused Mackay, 'could be a series of coincidences, but why and how did he get Steadman's notebook?'

'Because Craven was shagging a secretary at Parker & Co, his old employers,' she said excitedly, pointing to some clear lettering amidst the jumble of squiggles and dashes.

'The dirty bastard.'

'Shagging and impregnating by the look of it. There was a child,' said Sally, reading further on.

'The dirty bastard,' repeated Mackay.

'Craven's wife's family were devout Catholics and pillars of the local community, this would have been a scandal. Things have changed a lot since the early 60s but this still won't go down well with the Barnes and West Putney Blue Rinse Brigade. No wonder Penny Gray was pissed off when she found out he was getting his leg over at work. He maybe pushed her off the cliff to keep her quiet. This certainly gives him a motive, but it doesn't mean he killed her.'

'No.'

'I wonder what happened to the baby.'

'I don't know and I don't care, but we'll no doubt soon be seeing pictures of it in the Borough Gazette.'

'What shall we do?'

'Nothing. We do nothing. We wait for Steadman to turn up - then compare notes with him. This doesn't seem to be related to Gibraltar in any way.'

'No it doesn't,' she said, stifling a yawn.

'Listen, these hieroglyphics are giving me a headache. Why don't we drop it for now and go and grab something to eat?'

'No can do lover,' replied Sally. 'I'm off out with the girls tonight.'

'Oh,' mouthed a surprised Mackay, 'where are you off to?'

'The Flicks.'

'To see what?'

'The Full Monty of course, can't miss a full frontal of Robert Carlyle now, can I?'

Mackay caught up with her as she opened the door and he barely managed to squeeze in a kiss. 'Well, I'll see you tomorrow in the office then,' he said glumly, 'and Sal?'

'What?'

'Don't forget to vote.'

She turned to face him and gave him one of her genuine smiles. 'Rest assured Thomas - I'll be cancelling your vote out.' And then she left.

Mackay briefly stood still, staring at the closed door. If good, honest, professional women like Ms Purcell - born and bred in the Home Counties - were all voting for Blair, what hope was there?

There was a knock at the door.

Mackay walked towards it, glad that Sally had changed her mind - a full frontal of himself apparently proving more appealing than Robert Carlyle. He flung the door open and instinctively flinched backwards as the first of two men threw a massive punch at his stomach. Mackay hadn't recoiled far enough and the blow connected. He yelled and doubled over, completely winded. He heard the door close just as the second strike landed on his neck, spreading intense pain through his entire body. He screamed and crumpled to the floor, curling up into a ball as the blows rained down on him.

After two or three seconds he sensed his assailants' frustration, as although he was hurting all over they were failing to inflict any real damage with their punches. This prompted them to change tack and they began to kick him relentlessly. It was only then that Mackay, probably for the first time in his adult life, began to feel frightened - truly terrified. He'd seen that the men were wearing balaclavas. Were they just softening him up before they robbed him, or was it worse? Was this it? Game over?'

'What the fuck's this,' screamed a drunken voice in a harsh Edinburgh accent. The kicking stopped and Mackay turned to catch a glimpse of Big Rab Anderson out of the corner of his eye.

The Fat Man was naked save for his saltire boxer shorts, over which spilled the enormous belly that wobbled with an indented ripple. Rab was fiery at the best of times, but in a situation like this - and booze fuelled - he was incandescent with rage. The bloodlust conveyed by his bleary red eyes was not lost on the two assailants who crucially hesitated to face the onslaught from their flank. Mackay was glad that he'd left his golf clubs propped against the banister at the foot of the stairs as he saw his nine iron crash into the balaclava of the leading intruder with a soft thud. The stroke would have hooked the ball right out of bounds on the 1st at Royal Burgess - no doubt eliciting a ripple of laughter from the more observant members sitting in the clubhouse - but undeterred Rab played his second more like a bunker shot, catching the intruder under the chin with an almighty thwack as he followed through. As a contest the encounter was over and the intruders began to edge back towards the door - continually parrying the blows from the flailing nine iron as they went.

Mackay got to his feet and positioned himself off Rab's left shoulder - taking care to avoid the back swing from the whirling golf club. He ached all over and he was badly bruised in places but he knew that nothing was seriously wrong with him. He watched as the leading intruder managed to get both hands around the face of the club - nullifying its offensive capability - but this allowed Rab to control the upper part of the staff with his right hand, whilst using his left fist to smash into the man's completely unprotected face. The man's head snapped backwards and he semi-pirouetted into his colleague who bundled him out into the street. By the time Rab had reached the outside step, they were out of sight.

As the compliance officer stood framed by the open door, Mackay could see that his back was wet with sweat. He turned to face Mackay and discharged a couple of boar like snorts in his general direction before slamming the door shut. Then Rab flung the nine iron on the floor and plunged onto the sofa, he was exhausted. Mackay saw that his briefcase containing Steadman's notebook had gone.

'Well, that's one way…' Rab wheezed. 'Of…sobering…' Rab paused to exhale loudly. 'Up,' he said, breathing out noisily again.

There was silence as the two Scotsmen turned over the whole unpleasant experience in their minds. Having got his breath back, it was Rab who spoke first. 'Who the hell were they?'

'Fuck knows,' replied Mackay, dwelling on what might have been if the fat oaf on the sofa next to him had not been at a conference at the Barbican that day. He thought about his attackers. Were they two hungry asylum seekers intent on robbery, or was this anything to do with Craven trying to get the notebook back?

'Anything broken?' asked Rab, trying to sound compassionate.

'Just a few bruises.'

'Listen, I know the police have given up on muggings and robbery in this shite city, but that was serious - those guys need to be locked up.'

'More likely deported,' replied Mackay.

'Whatever, I think you should call the rozzers anyway.'

Mackay nodded, and then walked slowly through to the kitchen, gingerly testing his sore muscles as he went. He returned with two cold lagers and sat next to Rab on the sofa.

Mackay told him of his suspicions about Craven, Platt's death, Bridger's near admission of guilt and the scandal involving the Atlantic and General Trading Company. Rab sat still and silent throughout, snorting occasionally, gulping his lager, not interrupting. After he had finished, Mackay paused, rubbing his neck where the most painful blow had fallen. 'Well, what do you think?'

Rab hesitated before answering, his face knotted together as if contemplating some complex theorem. Finally he turned on the sofa to face Mackay.

'What a load of bollocks - you always were a fantasist.'

'Yes, you're right. Whether Craven's involved or not is irrelevant. That was scary. Shall I call Inspector Steele or the local police?'

'I would call Steele,' replied Rab, 'you'll get a better response from him if he thinks it's linked to Everyman.'

Mackay signalled his agreement with this suggestion by picking up his wallet from the mantelpiece. If his attackers had been robbers, thought Mackay, surely they would have taken his wallet? He found Inspector Steele's card and called the number on it.

'Can I speak to Inspector Steele please...would you mind asking him to call Tom Mackay when he gets in...yes, he knows what it's about.' Mackay put the phone down and returned to the sofa.

'Right. I'm off for a shower,' said Rab, 'got to look my best for the fleshpots of the capital.'

Rab left the room and Mackay reached for the remote control. He switched on Channel 4 News and saw pictures of the Prime Minister being pelted with eggs during a visit to Stevenage. The mob was more aggressive than the one which he'd seen outside Clapham Junction earlier. But this time the skirmish was more even because Mr Major's Special Branch officers were clearly experienced at keeping away the very determined Marxists who were trying to get close to him. The phone rang and Mackay picked it up.

'Tom Mackay?' said a voice smoothly.

'Yes.'

'Alex Williams.' The caller needed no further introduction - he was the Senior Partner of Blake and Lander. 'Tom, I'll come straight to the point. I understand that one or two issues have arisen on the audit you're currently undertaking, Everyman Credit, would I be right?'

'That's right Alex,' replied Mackay, as evenly as he could manage.

'I'd like to offer you my help.' The Senior Partner then stopped speaking and adjusted his tone of voice from smooth to velvety. 'Would you like me to help you?'

'Yes.'

'That's excellent. Why don't you come and see me first thing tomorrow morning, say 8.30. Do you know where my office is?'

'Yes.' Mackay then thought he heard whispering at the other end of the line. 'If I'm to help you Tom, it's best not to involve any external parties at this stage, keep it all intra-firm for now until we decide what's best to do. Don't you agree?'

'Yes, if you think that's best Alex.'

'I do, Tom, I do. In fact Tom, I wouldn't even mention our meeting to Silas Craven for the moment. Let's see where we all stand before we bring him in shall we?'

'OK Alex.'

'Fine, tomorrow at 8.30 then,' and before Mackay could respond he'd hung up.

Mackay went to the fridge and got himself another lager. He returned to the living room and sat down on the sofa. How had Williams found out about Everyman? Were they planning to throw him to the wolves or would there be some sort of pay-off offered? It was significant that Craven hadn't been invited. It was well known that there was no love lost between Williams and Craven as a result of the bitter succession battle a few years ago. But surely Williams couldn't cut Craven loose - Craven knew where too many of the bodies were buried. There was no doubt now that the insurance fraud was genuine, but how far did it go - murder? Mackay was still puzzling over how Williams had managed to unearth Everyman when the phone rang for a second time. It was Inspector Steele.

'Mr Mackay?'

'Yes.'

'It's Inspector Steele. You left a message for me earlier.'

'Er, yes Inspector,' stuttered Mackay, using a mouthful of beer as a device to buy time whilst he thought what he was going to say. Since the call from Williams, Mackay had gone off the idea of sharing his experiences of the last hour with the policeman. And he had also decided against burdening the Inspector with his foolish conspiracy theories, at least until he had a chance to meet with Williams the following day.

'Have I caught you in the middle of your supper?'

'No, just an early beer,' replied Mackay, loudly clearing his throat, what could he say?

'What is it then?'

'Not much I'm afraid, probably not important, just something that one of the girls in the office said.'

'Who in the office?'

'Sally Purcell.'

'Yes, go on.'

'Well, she said that Keith had said that something was odd with the Everyman audit.' Mackay immediately regretted using the word odd, and instantly attempted to backtrack. 'When I say odd, what I mean is an unresolved audit issue.'

'I see. Have you found anything odd yourself?'

'No,' said Mackay robustly, but then he added, 'but I haven't finished it yet.' It was best to keep his options open should tomorrow's meeting with Williams prove to be unfruitful.

'Do you know Sally Purcell well Mr Mackay?' said Steele.

'Yes.'

'Were you screwing her before Keith Platt's death sir?' asked the Inspector, making the question sound criminal, sordid and condemning. It caught Mackay by surprise and threw him off balance.

'No I was not,' stammered Mackay forcefully. 'Look, what is

this Steele?' The policeman didn't answer the question, but instead asked another one himself.

'Where were you yesterday evening sir?' It was the 'sir' part of the question which alarmed Mackay the most. The policeman had always called him Mr Mackay or Tom, never sir, the use of the word concerned him.

'I was at a Tory Party meeting in Putney,' said Mackay quickly.

'Many people there sir?'

'At least a dozen. Commander Roper, he's the agent, he'll confirm it.' Mackay pressed his ear against the phone but could only hear the general office hubbub coming from the other end. 'What is this Inspector?'

'Your client, Jonathan Bridger, he died last night.'

Mackay was stunned. Surely this was foul play. He glanced at his front door to make sure that it was on the latch. 'How?' he said weakly.

'Problem with his gas fire. He was well into his second bottle of Scotch so I doubt if he knew much about it. Seems the flame blew out, it was lucky there wasn't an explosion.'

Mackay imagined Bridger slumped back on his sofa in a drunken stupor, oblivious to Craven hovering over the gas fire switching the tap off and on.

'You see my dilemma Mr Mackay,' continued the Inspector more gently, 'too many coincidences here for me. My boss on the other hand - she's the department's budget-holder - she has a more favourable view of coincidences than me. A hit and run driver, a domestic accident, it happens all the time, but to two connected individuals within a month - I don't buy it. And I warn you now, and this is the only warning you'll get from me. If I find out that you've held anything back, anything at all, I'll be after you, and I won't let go. I don't like threatening decent professional folk like yourself, but sometimes it's necessary.'

Mackay suspected the opposite was true but he decided against debating the point with the Inspector.

'Is there anything you'd like to add to what you've just told me?' said Steele.

'No,' replied Mackay resolutely.

'OK then sir. I'd be obliged if you would stay in London until further notice. No more dirty weekends in Gibraltar without my permission.'

Steele hung up before Mackay could reply. He wasn't sure whether he was more shocked by the news of Bridger's death or by the fact that Steele knew he'd been to Gibraltar with Sally. He instantly regretted not coming clean with the policeman. The situation was getting out of hand and Steele could protect him. Sure, there might be benefits arising from tomorrow's meeting with Williams, but it was more than that, he wasn't entirely convinced himself that these deaths weren't coincidences. He heard Rab come out of the shower upstairs and head for the guest bedroom. One thing was for certain, he wouldn't be leaving the side of that fearsome warrior this evening.

CHAPTER 16

(THURSDAY 1ST MAY 1997 - ELECTION DAY)

DON'T GIVE UP ON US SAYS MAJOR
BLAIR GIVES HIS ALL ON THE LAST DAY OF THE CAMPAIGN
OUR KIND OF GUY, SINATRA IS, SAYS CONGRESS

Despite his earlier promise to himself, Mackay had left Rab at midnight and travelled back to Putney alone by cab. He'd seen that the West End had been busier than usual and mobbed with City Traders having a last drink under the Ancien Regime. During the evening Rab had pursued an unlicensed Kiwi nightmare named Rebecca, and whilst Mackay had been prepared to provide some support as Wingman, his main priority was to stay fresh and alert for his meeting with Williams the following day.

Consequently, he was up and out before anyone else had stirred. He had a smooth commute into the City and he was at No.1 Westmorland Park by 8.15. The building was the grandest of the four sites the firm had in London and befit the distinguished senior accountants who inhabited the luxurious recesses of its upper floors.

Mackay had been in the building once before and only then to attend a presentation on the ground floor. Accordingly, he couldn't find the lifts. And he soon found himself wandering through the semi-dark kitchens in the basement, where - whilst fumbling for the light switch - he knocked into a heavily laden hostess trolley. This sent a variety of plates and cutlery crashing noisily onto the tiled floor. Fortunately, this clattering alerted one of the security guards who appeared from nowhere and directed him to a dimly lit bay where the service lift was hidden. Christ, no wonder I couldn't find these, thought Mackay, as he got in and pressed the button for the seventh floor.

The lift door opened onto a screened ante-room. Mackay walked through the ante-room and into a reception area where he noticed the main lifts stood. There was a library-like hush on the floor and a sweet smell of flowers, possibly the real thing, thought Mackay, but a second sniff suggested chemicals and an up-market plug-in. If the firm's interior designer had intended to recreate a sumptuous Edwardian meet and greet area then she'd certainly succeeded. The ornate wood panelling was exquisitely carved, the plush mauve carpet was thick pile, and the glittering chandeliers were pure Titanic. And, in the midst of it all, sat the most gorgeous blue eyed blonde he'd seen all year.

The Vision had noticed Mackay's arrival by the service lift, so her smile was not the one which she gave to visiting Captains of Industry. What she was doing manning the seventh floor reception desk of Blake and Lander was beyond him. Here was a girl destined for the catwalk. Perhaps she's only got one leg, he thought, toying with the idea of glancing over the lip of the desk as he approached. But as he got closer, even her third tier smile proved too much for him. He instructed his tongue to emit speech but no response came. After a couple of seconds of wordless flapping Mackay eventually managed to blurt out, 'Alex Williams please.' She smiled at him again, second tier this time, and gestured towards a green leather sofa which sat under huge Victorian photographs of Mr Blake and Mr Lander.

Mackay sat down and picked up one of the FTs which lay on the occasional table adjacent to the sofa. May as well look keen, he thought, as he stole a furtive glance at the receptionist. She was at right angles to him now, and when he'd unfolded the FT fully he was able to peek over the top and ogle her at his leisure. From his hide, he saw a slender white arm appear from under the desk and reach for the phone.

'Tom Mackay to see you,' chirped The Vision sweetly. There was a muffled reply from the other end and she replaced the handset on the cradle. Mackay flicked through the FT looking at the pictures. It was hot, and soon the paper began to have a hypnotic effect on him and he started to feel drowsy. He began to drift into a trance like state, and he was unable to resist when the attractive receptionist soon appeared as a guest fantasy.

Moments later the sound of a heavy door opening jolted him into full consciousness and he sprang to his feet - sending the FT cart-wheeling to the floor. He looked up and she smiled at him, her first tier smile somehow seeming to legitimise his fantasy. He stooped to pick up the paper and so was unable to shake Alex Williams hand when he straightened up. The Senior Partner stood motionless whilst Mackay awkwardly transferred the paper to his left hand, freeing up his right.

'Thanks very much for coming to see me at such short notice, Tom, shall we go into my office.'

Mackay followed the king of the firm through the heavy oak doors and into the throne room. Mackay was impressed with what he saw. Williams's desk was framed by an enormous floor to ceiling window through which Mackay could see the grey brown water of the Thames and London Bridge in the distance. In stark contrast to the windowless reception area, this room was filled with natural light. Whereas the previous room had been stuffy, this office was airy and modern. There was an equally large mahogany table at the far end of the room at which sat four grey haired courtiers. There was a fifth man who was about Mackay's age sitting at the end of the table with an open note book in front of him, pen poised.

Williams headed for the chair at the other end of the table and invited Mackay to sit next to him. Mackay took the chair, clasped his hands together, and sat back. If the Gestapo like positioning of Williams and the courtiers had been intended to intimidate him, it had failed. He felt unusually relaxed and under-awed by the situation - strangely at ease with himself.

He looked more closely at Williams and saw one of those square pugnacious stocky types, balding but trim looking, more nightclub bruiser than accountant, his manner an unstable blend of affability and menace. Yesterday Mackay would have been fearful, but after last night's run-in with the Balaclava Boys, he didn't give a shit.

Williams looked at him without seeing him. Here was merely a minor ailment that needed treatment. The medication would be a simple course of monetary doses combined with a promotion and the raising of career expectations. Every man had his price and Williams suspected that this man's price wouldn't be high, although Mackay's careless body language and clear lack of deference had begun to concern him. Indeed, the man before him was *so* self-assured that Williams was tempted to drop the agreed strategy and adopt a more conciliatory tactic from the outset. A loud yawn from Mackay convinced him of this, so Williams sat back in his chair and threw his hands around his head.

'Are we keeping you up Tom?' beamed the Bruiser insincerely.

'Sorry Alex,' replied Mackay, 'late night on the stump.' Out of his peripheral vision Mackay noticed the four courtiers follow William's lead and simultaneously recline. The manoeuvre was embarrassing for all concerned and reminded Mackay of the Siamese children in the King and I. Mackay stifled a smirk and Williams looked away from the Gang of Four as he continued.

'Yes, I understand you've been helping get our own Silas Craven elected,' said Williams, glad that he'd been unexpectedly handed an easy lead into the main topic of the day.

'That's right,' replied Mackay, 'the seat's been Tory since 1905, so it shouldn't be difficult.'

'Excellent. Excellent.' The Senior Partner brought his hands from behind his head and leaned forward slightly in his chair.

Mackay couldn't resist glancing to his right but there was no response from the Gang of Four and they remained fully reclined. The fifth man put his pen to his notebook and Mackay sensed the exchange of pleasantries about the election was over.

'Well you know why I've asked you here Tom, perhaps you could tell us in your own words what's been going on down at Everyman. Please speak freely - we're all colleagues here.'

Mackay doubted whether they were all on the same team and he regretted not having an ally with him. But despite this he gave the room a full report of the Everyman audit, his views, his opinions and his suspicions. His thoughts on Bridger's death had induced a bout of fidgeting amongst the Gang of Four which didn't stop despite Mackay qualifying what he'd said with caveats about a lack of evidence etc. During the course of his diatribe it became clear to Mackay that Williams already knew much of what he said. Each extra piece of information elicited a further grimace from the Senior Partner whose screwed up face was gradually contorting into some sort of fleshy Kleenex. Mackay sensed that William's earlier geniality was gone, and he felt that the Bruiser would soon lash out at the nearest target, which was of course him. Years of practice, however, had taught Williams how to control his emotions, so when he continued, his voice was calm and even.

'As you say Tom, no hard evidence and a lot of speculation on your part. Serious allegations these. Allegations against a senior figure in this firm and a respected member of the financial community. For fuck's sake! This time tomorrow the man's likely to be an MP.' Williams stopped to flick open a slim leather folder that was on his desk in front of him.

Mackay could see that it was his own personnel file.

'The thing is what to do Tom, for a start it's possible that investing the insurance rebate in property was authorised by senior management at the Bank. In fact, that very thing has been suggested to me by Southern and London themselves. It's difficult to see how fraud has been committed in those circumstances.'

Clever, thought Mackay, with Bridger gone there was nothing to contradict such an assertion.

'I can see how it would have been easy to miss this,' continued Williams gently, 'you clearly weren't aware that the documentation supporting this transaction was held at Group. I'm sure most of us would have failed to spot it.' Williams smiled at him in an understanding way, but the threat was clear. 'The three deaths you've mentioned, Vassallo, Platt, Bridger. One a drunken suicide, another a hit and run and the third a gas leak. All tenuously linked, yes - but over a period of thirty years. And each murdered by Silas Craven, preposterous. I've known the man for twenty five years myself.'

'There's the journalist as well,' volunteered Mackay.

'He'll turn up. He hasn't even been reported missing, has he?' It was now clear that Williams was intending to bury the whole Everyman stench down a three hundred foot concrete lined silo. The only outstanding issue was Mackay. Would he scurry in behind the rapidly closing ranks of the firm, or squeal to Inspector Steele?

'Now Tom, I really value the work that you've done on this job. It's been difficult, senior staff have departed from our procedures, guidelines haven't been followed, misjudgements have been made. Do you know what this is?'

'It looks like my personnel file.'

'It is. It is. To be frank Tom it's not stellar is it?'

'No. I haven't felt particularly challenged in recent years Alex.'

'No. Well, as I said Tom, you've done well on this job, very well. So well in fact that I think you're ready for more responsibility. How about promotion with immediate effect - a battlefield promotion as it were?' Williams glanced at Mackay to gauge his reaction but Mackay sat impassively. Williams had expected some sort of response but Mackay didn't give one, so the Senior Partner continued. 'Of course there's the issue of your bonuses. I see from here that you've never had one despite being eligible for the last four years. I'm sure that we can see our way to putting that right and backdating this year's to '93. That would add up to quite a tidy sum.'

Mackay had done the maths before Williams had finished speaking. It was forty eight grand. Mackay could see that Williams didn't find negotiating with him demeaning in any way. To him Mackay merely represented a problem that needed to be solved, this was just business. Mackay was pleased with the generosity of the proposed pay off but surprised when Williams went further.

'Of course, individuals like you Tom, who show exceptional loyalty to Blake and Lander, can, in time, be expected to reach the very highest levels of the firm.'

Mackay looked at the Gang of Four and imagined himself joining their ranks. He began to realise that he had a stronger hand than he'd thought, so he decided to chance his arm.

'That would depend on what 'in time' meant Alex.'

'Four, five years at the most. Certainly during my watch anyway. Of course, further progression would depend on your absolute commitment to the firm Tom.' Williams paused. 'Are you committed?'

'I am committed,' replied Mackay, as if swearing an oath to some ancient Masonic sect.

'Oh, that is good,' said Williams, giving Mackay the same plastic smile that Craven used. Did the firm purchase plastic smiles wholesale he wondered? Mackay half expected applause from the Gang of Four but instead they got up when Williams did and advanced to shake Mackay's hand.

After a minute or two of meaningless small talk Williams took Mackay by the arm and guided him to the heavy oak door. As Williams put his hand on the shiny brass handle and opened the door he turned to Mackay, 'I do appreciate your candour and commitment Tom, you leave the Everyman loose ends to me.' He reached into his jacket pocket and brought out a silver card holder, 'any problems, any problems at all, please call me directly on this number. I'll see that Jane puts you straight through.'

Mackay couldn't help giving a deferential nod as he turned to head for the lifts, but he then realized that Williams had held onto his arm. The Senior Partner casually tightened his grip and brought his face six inches from Mackay's. Williams glanced at the iconic pictures of Mr Blake and Mr Lander and squeezed hard. 'This firm's been operating for over one hundred and twenty years now Tom. It's a great firm, an institution in fact, and nothing but nothing is going to jeopardise its future. Not on my watch, not on anybody's watch. Do I make myself clear?'

'I understand Alex,' replied Mackay, as resolutely as he could manage, 'I fully understand.'

'Excellent,' he said, releasing both his grip and his intense stare, 'that's excellent,' and Williams then spun round and returned to his office.

Mackay stole one last glance at the attractive receptionist then headed for the main lifts.

CHAPTER 17

(THURSDAY 1ST MAY 1997 - THE SAME DAY)

From the corner of the sixth floor Junior's Room in Wessex Court, Craven had an uninterrupted view of No. 1 Westmorland Park. He had stood in the empty room for some time, watching, watching until he saw Mackay come out of the main door and cross the road. He shrank into the wall as he saw Mackay walk stiffly towards him, then disappear through the door below. Mackay had clearly been in pain and Craven regretted that last night's attempt to scare him had got out of hand. He heard the phone ring in his office across the corridor and he ran to pick it up. It was Alex Williams.

'Silas.'

'Yes.'

'He's taken it.'

'Good... and Southern and London?'

'They're on board. John Llewellyn is a member of my club. He's got someone at Group to sign off on a document authorising a loan to Bridger for the few hundred thousand he actually borrowed. The same document also instructs Bridger to invest the balance of the seven million off-shore.'

'Will it wash?'

'It's hardly material is it? And who's going to spot it anyway? We're the fucking auditors aren't we? Now you listen to me Silas,' said Williams fiercely. 'Mackay made some serious allegations about you in here - you keep a lid on them. Do you understand me? If I hear anything else about this it'll be you who falls off a rock.'

'That was an accident,' replied Craven, but Williams had already hung up.

Four floors below, Mackay sat at his desk aimlessly flicking through a file, too excited to concentrate. Tony King, seeing Mackay's lack of productivity, felt obliged to comment.

'You busy then?'

'You know me Tony, continually generating fees for the firm, I'm a money machine, I am.'

'Certainly looks that way,' said King sarcastically.

Mackay looked up from his desk and couldn't resist a swipe. 'Bet you a hundred quid I'm promoted before you.'

King snorted. He, Mackay, everyone knew that the staff weren't told about their promotions until August. It was common knowledge that he was next in line after Platt, and with Platt gone, King's promotion was a certainty. What was Mackay thinking of - he wasn't even in the running.

'Try two hundred.'

Mackay got up from his desk and stood opposite King and shook his hand. 'You're on.' An easy two hundred thought Mackay. Then it struck him that the major benefit of his promotion would be a move towards the senior end of the building, which would of course mean, sadly, an end to his cohabitation with the delightful King.

Given that Mackay's new patron was none other than the Senior Partner, he felt largely immune from any Departmental authority, and naturally disinclined to do any work whatsoever. He felt a sense of liberation, and he determined to test out his new found freedom by immediately adjourning to the King Lud for an early lunch.

The pub was packed with the bedrock of the outgoing government, city traders, investment bankers and fund managers - all drowning their sorrows and clinging to the hope of a ballot box miracle. Well-heeled corporate lawyers jostled with fat tax advisors for space at the bar. Whilst a dozen Basildon men crowded noisily around a fruit machine in the corner - swigging lager out of branded bottles with every spin of the wheels. Mackay spotted some fellow Blake and Lander journeymen seated on the dais at the far end of the pub and joined them.

By the time he lurched back to his office four hours later, it was clear that his largely liquid lunch had rendered him incapable of any meaningful bean counting. He decided to call it a day and clear his desk, which he did by opening the large drawer at the bottom and sweeping everything into it using the full length of his arm. He kicked the drawer closed and grabbed forcefully at his jacket, a quiet ripping sound indicating that he'd failed to unhook it properly before pulling.

As he approached the door on his way out, Tony King appeared carrying a vending cup. Mackay swerved to miss him but overcorrected to avoid the bin and caught him on the elbow. The contents of the cup sprayed in a two hundred and seventy degree arc, drenching King, and leaving a basketball sized stain over his shirt and groin. A quick scan of Mackay's own clothes revealed that he'd found the only dry quadrant.

When King realised this it intensified his rage, and he flung the empty tomato soup cup at Mackay's back as he left the room. The cup missed and hit the cream wall on the other side of the corridor, creating an orange polka dot effect worthy of Laurence Llewellyn-Bowen.

'You bastard,' shouted King, but Mackay was already in the lift.

Mackay decided to take the train rather than the tube, hoping that the walk to Waterloo would sober him up. Although he did feel a little fresher as he got on, the carriage was hot, and by Clapham Junction he'd dozed off, waking only when the train terminated at Richmond. By the time he had caught another train back to Putney, voted, and walked to the flat, it had gone 5.00. A further short nap and a lukewarm shower completed the sobering up process, and having changed into his election uniform, he headed for Balfour Street.

It was a warm, pleasant evening, and the sight of Roper fidgeting nervously outside the office couldn't detract from it. Mackay noticed that all the windows on the second floor flat now displayed large, bright, 'Vote Labour' posters, whereas the blue flaming torches on the ground floor were dog-eared and faded.

'Lovely evening Lawrence,' beamed Mackay.

'Make the most of it Tom,' said the agent, 'the sun won't shine again under Labour.'

'Do I finally detect a note of defeatism?'

'Just reality. We'll be alright here of course, but the exit polls from the marginals aren't good. I won't stay you know.'

'The holiday home in Madeira?' enquired Mackay.

'Not big enough. I'll sell up here and buy something bigger on the island. The market's probably peaked here anyway - can't see people wanting to invest in property in the UK when they've got rubbish and dead folk piling up on their doorsteps.'

'Mmm….,' mused Mackay. 'I'll be off as well if it gets that bad. There's no end of secondment opportunities in Australia.'

'But you can't leave Tom,' said Roper energetically, 'someone needs to keep the flame burning. It's time the younger generation took over from Old Farts like me anyway. Here's a thought, why don't you take over from me, as agent I mean. You know Silas, you're good with people, you've got more of a lateral view than most of the automatons who work here. Then when Silas retires, you'd be in pole position to take over.'

Mackay was stunned.

'Well I'm flattered Lawrence.' Mackay realised that from an external point of view his relationship with Craven must look good, although - unbeknown to Roper - Mackay half suspected him of murder. Mackay was saved from any further unexpected (and unwarranted) praise from Roper by Annabel. Who appeared at the door in Mackay's favourite black polo shirt, which, as usual, struggled to keep her fully housed.

'Silas is on his way Commander,' she said.

'Right, OK,' said Roper, snapping back into military mode, 'let's head over to the Recreation centre.'

'Anything more for me to do Lawrence?' asked Mackay. 'I'll be there for the declaration of course - only I've got a date.'

The question was directed at Roper but intended for Annabel. Mackay was pleased to see her flinch slightly, and when she spoke her voice lacked its usual careless confidence.

'Tommy's got a date,' she said, 'anybody we know?'

'A girl from the office, I'll bring her along tonight.'

'Does she bat for us?' asked Roper.

'I doubt it,' replied Mackay, 'at best a floater.'

'Well bring her along to our…er…celebrations. I think the declaration will be about oneish.' Roper turned and went back into the building. Before following him in, Annabel caught Mackay's eye, she looked at him for a couple of seconds - her mouth slightly open - and then she tightened her lips as if to speak but instead exhaled heavily through her nose. Then she was gone.

Always the way with women, thought Mackay, as soon as you were off the market they were interested. He wondered whether his relationship with Sally was informal enough to allow further exploration of this first sign of interest from Annabel. Naturally, the ideal situation would be a simultaneous sexual relationship with both of them. This could be achieved and justified during some sort of vague and lengthy overlap period, after which he could take his pick, probably Sally. Pleasurable images of breakfast with Sally followed by evening cocoa with Annabel filled his mind. He had already seen the flimsy number which passed for Sally's occasional nightie. What would Annabel wear? One of his shirts perhaps, or maybe a long but easily accessible nightdress - a hang up from her boarding school days. The prospect of pulling either off Annabel's curvaceous body was mouth-watering, and it was this image that fixed in his mind.

He was surprised that when he sat down at Sally's table in the High Street Wine Bar shortly afterwards, he could still only see Annabel. Was his libido trying to tell him something? Sally was dressed in a blue business suit with a white shirt wide open at the neck. She gave him a hard look and he noticed that she'd almost finished a large glass of chardonnay.

'Where've you been?'
'I'm not late am I?'
'You know I don't like to be kept waiting.'
'I had important party business to take care of.'
'Get me another drink.'
Mackay walked to the bar and ordered a large white wine, and, as there was no draught bitter, a bottle of Becks. He returned to the table where he sensed a thaw.
'Show me your bruises then.'
He lifted his shirt to parade the purplest one which was located under his right rib cage. She jabbed it with her finger and he flinched in pain.
'Bloody Hell Sal.'
'Certainly looks painful,' she said, attempting a second jab.
Mackay caught her finger and held it tightly.
'Well, what are we going to do about Silas?' continued Sally, distracting him long enough to free her finger.
'Do? We're going to do nothing. Williams will have told Silas by now that I've been bought off. Silas will call off his thugs. He'll get elected. I'll be promoted and get a large bonus. The good name of Blake and Lander won't be dragged through the mud. The merger between Southern and Caledonian will be a success, and…' He paused. '… I get the girl.'
'What about Keith, Bridger, and that journalist?'
'Nick Steadman will turn up. Bridger's death was an accident or suicide, and Keith's was a hit and run.'
She took a large gulp out of her glass and he drained the rest of his bottle. 'Very neat and tidy.'
'It is if you take the Mackay view,' he said, slightly slurring his words, 'I'm a company man now you know.' The strong lager had reacted with the latent alcohol from his earlier half gallon of bitter, and he suddenly felt quite drunk.
'Listen Sal, why don't we get a takeaway pizza and head back to the flat. Nothing's going to happen until the early hours and we could catch the start of the election coverage on the telly.'
She glanced over to the group of teenagers in the corner who

were becoming increasingly boisterous with every mouthful of Hooch. They had been amusing to begin with, but now they were irritating.

'Ok,' she said, 'this bar's overrun with youths now anyway - it's not what it was. Let's be adults and go watch politics.'

'Great,' said Mackay, getting to his feet, his mind dwelling on other adult activities that could be pursued only at home.

Of the two Dimblebys, Mackay found David the more tolerable, so despite its clear left wing bias they watched the BBC. It was fortunate for Dimbleby that the TV in Mackay's flat was not two way, as the Broadcaster would surely have been distracted from describing each new Labour gain by the x-rated display which took place on the sofa a few feet away from his flickering face. Mackay found it difficult to concentrate on anything other than the matter in hand, but when he heard Dimbleby describe the loss of Birmingham Edgbaston, and then Crosby, with an eighteen percent swing to Labour, he looked up.

'Bloody hell - this is a meltdown, we haven't won a seat yet, even Craven could be in trouble.'

'For God's sake, Tom, switch that off and please finish what you're doing.'

The 5-a-side football hall at the Heath Recreation Centre was as full as it had been on the night of 'Question Time,' though now the seats in which the general public had sat were replaced with long tables at which tellers perched, counting voting papers. Rather than noise there was an excitable buzz around the hall, the only distinguishable voice being that of Roper.

Mackay had known as soon as they'd arrived that opening the second bottle of Chardonnay had been a mistake. The occasion clearly demanded a degree of gravitas, which both he and Sally were now completely incapable of giving. Mackay tried to look serious as Geoff bounded up to him, his blue rosette spinning round like a half drunken propeller.

'It's bad Tom, that's their pile and that's ours.' Mackay looked across the room at the two even piles of ballot papers, if anything; the pile on the left looked slightly larger.

'Which one's ours?'

'The one on the right.'

'Geoff, this is Sally Purcell, a close friend of mine.'

'Nice to meet you Sally, sorry, must dash.'

'Clearly an important man,' giggled Sally.

'Our Geoff doesn't get out much, it means a lot to him this result.' Mackay could see Craven at the far end of the hall by the edge of a platform where he assumed the declaration would take place. He stood motionless, standing tall above Roper, Annabel, and the other party workers who busied themselves around him doing God knows what. Craven was looking at Sally but then he caught Mackay's eye and acknowledged him with a lazy flicker of his eyelid. To Craven's left, a fat balding man who Mackay remembered as the local government officer turned trades unionist trouble maker - the Labour candidate Paul Smith - was locked in conversation with Roger Metcalfe. Behind them was the Liberal candidate, who did nothing other than stand and smile. And to his right was the Returning Officer, who began tapping on the microphone in the middle of the platform. Having completed his sound check, he straightened himself up and cleared his throat.

'Er...hello everyone, we're just about to finish the count, I'll give the result in five to ten minutes.' The announcement made no impact on the Liberal, UKIP or Green candidates, they were also-rans, but Mackay saw Paul Smith began to fiddle with his red rosette and even Craven looked nervous.

They were ten long minutes. Mackay saw the Returning Officer consult, then re-consult with his staff, then consult again. A few more papers were added to the Smith pile and then to Craven's, then Smith's. All of the candidates drifted towards the platform.

'Shall we join your colleagues?' asked Sally.

'No, let's watch from here,' said Mackay with a smirk, 'isn't democracy wonderful?'

'I must say the candidates are very representative,' said Sally, 'five, white, middle aged men.'

'You'll be in favour of quotas of course, all women lists.'

'I might be if this is typical of most constituencies.'

The Returning Officer opened his hand and indicated that the candidates should join him on the platform. They filed past him and stood facing the hall. All of them except the Liberal candidate, who continued to smile, looked very serious. There was a hush in the hall as the Returning Officer began to speak.

'I, Richard Mead, being the Returning Officer for the Barnes and West Putney constituency, declare that the votes cast in the general election in the said constituency are as follows; Christopher Bryant, UK Independence Party, one thousand seven hundred and six. Silas Craven, Conservative Party, twenty thousand four hundred and twelve. Colin Finch, Liberal Democrat, three thousand and twenty six. Jonathan Pardoe, Green Party, nine hundred and sixty seven.'

Mead paused theatrically, fiddled with the microphone, and cleared his throat. There was an impatient shuffling in the hall and a roar erupted from the Labour supporters around Smith. 'Paul Smith,' began Mead, but he had missed his chance, and he was drowned out by the escalating racket which now filled the whole hall. 'Paul Smith, the Labour Party candidate…,' but once more his voice was lost in the noise, as the Labour supporters started chanting, and all that could be heard above the generally din was ' Smithyeee… Smithyeee … Smithyeee … Smithyeee … Smithyeee … Smithyeee …Smithyeee, …'

'Quiet please,' cajoled Mead. 'Paul Smith, the Labour Party candidate, twenty thousand…' the chanting intensified but Mead decided to battle on, 'twenty thousand three hundred…'

Mackay saw Craven fling his arms up as Roper and Annabel took off and hugged each other mid-air. There was a stunned silence from the Labour ranks and Paul Smith looked even more crumpled than usual.

Mead hadn't finished. 'Twenty thousand, three hundred and forty four, and I hereby declare that Silas Anthony Craven has been duly elected to represent the parliamentary constituency of Barnes and West Putney.'

Roper began a round of thin applause which quickly died

down as Craven approached the microphone.

'I'd like to thank the police, my agent and his staff…'

'I can't listen to this,' said Mackay.

'Hardly a cause for celebration is it? A majority of eleven thousand reduced to around a hundred.'

'No Sal, it isn't. Let's go before we have to say something nice to the People's Representative.'

She took his hand and led him out of the hall. The reality of Craven's election slowly began to sink in. Surely there were supposed to be safeguards in the system which weeded out those who weren't fit for office? Mackay thought back to the succession of reprobates who had reached ministerial rank in the Major government and realised that any safeguards which did exist, were at best weak. New Labour would be the same but without the one core competency which pays for everything else, business experience. Over-promoted time served councillors and union officials, more self-serving lawyers than you could shake a stick at, media savvy journalists, the age of the professional politician had arrived. And it would herald more waste, bureaucracy and red tape, than those grey haired businessmen who were currently packing their bags around Whitehall could ever have imagined. Britain had been booming under the Tories - odd thing democracy, thought Mackay.

CHAPTER 18

(FRIDAY 2ND MAY 1997)

LABOUR LANDSLIDE
PORTILLO, FORSYTH, LANG ARE SWEPT AWAY IN ROUT
SLOWDOWN AS HOUSE PRICES TAKE BREATHER

When he walked into his office the next morning, Mackay saw that there was a yellow post-it note stuck to his computer. It read, 'Tom, please pop up to see me when you get in, Silas.'

As Mackay approached Craven's room on the sixth floor, he caught a glimpse of the same red braces which had acted as a hazard warning the previous month. The half packed boxes strewn across the room indicated that the new member for Barnes and West Putney had already begun the move to Westminster. Although Mackay doubted whether Craven would completely sever his links with the firm, as that would entail surviving solely on a MP's salary. Craven heard Mackay clip one of the boxes behind him and he spun round. He smiled at Mackay with his signature emotionless warmth, and gestured to him that he should sit down.

'You know I have to share an office with two others at Westminster?'

'How ever will you manage?' said Mackay, with unguarded sarcasm. Craven looked at him sharply, momentarily doubting his loyalty. There was a pause. And then Mackay thought it prudent to build bridges. 'Will you leave the firm altogether?'

'No. I'll remain as a consultant, besides, my overheads are too high to allow me to leave the private sector altogether. Wives are expensive you know.'

Mackay knew that Craven was trying to be light-hearted, trying to be nice to him, but it made both men feel uncomfortable. Mackay realised for the first time that he hated Craven, and he hoped that he would soon revert back to his usual default disdain, but instead the parliamentarian continued with the uneasy pleasantness.

'Listen Tom, I've asked you up here to thank you, to thank you for your support over…on…er… well… a number of fronts.'

Interesting way of putting it thought Mackay. Did 'a number of fronts' translate as relentlessly pounding the streets of Barnes wearing a blue rosette and acting as an unpaid cheerleader for the beleaguered Major? Or did it cover ignoring all manner of criminality, ranging from fraud to murder? Mackay looked at Craven. He was impossible to read. What was going on behind those grey lifeless eyes? Was Mackay living in a parallel universe to think that this man, this pillar of the financial community was somehow involved in murder? Well it *was* incredible.

'You weren't involved in the deaths of those people, were you, Silas?' As a minimum Mackay expected Craven to look away, or at least shift in his seat or clasp his hands together tightly. Instead he was motionless, his gaze fixed intensely on the bridge of Mackay's nose.

'No.'

Craven had clearly been expecting this question. He'd had time to prepare his answer and his body language for it. He gave nothing away. 'Anything else that you'd like to ask me Tom, anything else you'd like to get off your chest. I can see that you're troubled.'

Mackay was pleased that Craven had reverted to his icy norm. Mackay didn't answer so Craven continued.

'Alex Williams tells me you've a great future in this firm Tom, he has plans for you. I always knew you were partnership material, you're a player, you can think laterally, you can see the angles.'

'I'm not like you Silas.'
'You're more like me than you think.'
'Bollocks.'
Craven flinched at this and his mouth hardened, it was time to take Mackay down a peg or two. 'We've a lot in common, more in common than you think.'
'What do you mean by that?' said Mackay? But he knew where Craven was going.
'Sally Purcell for example.'
'You've slept with her?'
'No, not slept with her Tom,' Craven smiled broadly then wet his lips with the tip of his tongue, 'just screwed her in the toilet of a swanky Mayfair hotel.' Mackay winced, and then tried to look composed, but Craven had succeeded in wounding him.
'That was juvenile Silas,' said Mackay tensely, 'she's entitled to the odd mistake, all water under the bridge now anyway, all history.'
'Really, that's not what she said on Wednesday night, you know, when you thought she was at the cinema. I may have misheard her though - she obviously couldn't talk properly with my cock in her mouth.'
Mackay leapt forward and tried to grab Craven by the throat but the MP had brought up his knee and Mackay bounced off it and fell backwards towards the door. Mackay sprang up for a second assault but a voice from behind checked him.
'I'm sorry Silas. I'll get some of these boxes moved at once.' It was Craven's secretary.
Mackay skirted around her and left the room, only pausing to leave the words, 'I'll get you - you fucker!' hanging in the air.
There was no sign of Sally in the Department and following the tomato soup incident King had thankfully avoided conversation with him. By the time he was on the District Line heading west he had calmed down enough to gather his thoughts. To hell with them thought Mackay, to hell with them all. It *had* been the departmental rumour three years ago that Sally had gone off with Craven during the firm's Christmas Party at the Dorchester. Nothing had ever been proved or

admitted to, and at the time Mackay had been envious, but he hadn't cared then, now, he did. How had Craven known she'd been at the cinema on Wednesday? Was she seeing Craven? Had Mackay been completely deceived? It *had* surprised him how quickly she had ended up in his bed after Platt's death - but he had put this down to the convenience of a known shoulder to cry on and the twinkle in his eye. He thought back to Wednesday night when she had walked out of his flat moments before his two attackers had burst in. A coincidence, or was she Craven's spy as well as his lover? If Craven had intended to hurt him he'd certainly succeeded. Did he think Mackay would just take this and roll over, all for some poxy promotion and a forty eight grand bonus? Craven had miscalculated and now he would be punished.

Mackay arrived at Connaught House and went straight up to the third floor. Outside Bridger's office sat a very young and attractive brunette who had the bearing of a temp. Mackay sidled up to her desk and when she spoke she confirmed his assumption.

'Mrs Paterson's not in today - she's taken some time off. I'm Mandy, are you the auditor?'

'Yes.'

'I was told to expect you. There is a message for you from Inspector Steele. He said he'll be here at about eleven, and that if you were in, would you mind waiting for him.'

'Oh, thanks.' Mackay went into the Boardroom and pulled out the files. He had half expected them to have disappeared or at least to have been tampered with, but they all seemed to be how he had left them. He marked the incriminating pages with a post-it and pulled out the fax from Avon and General. This should be enough for Steele he thought.

He called Sally at home and at the office but she seemed to have disappeared. He knew that she would confirm what Craven had said about the Dorchester but he was desperate to hear from her about Wednesday night. He knew he wasn't being rational and that their relationship wasn't mature enough to have become exclusive. Indeed, only yesterday, he himself had contemplated having another pop at Annabel - but it was a primeval thing. Craven had deliberately acted like a Viking, thinking Mackay wouldn't retaliate, but he was wrong. Mackay suspected that Steele was keen to have a go at Craven, and that even if nothing stuck he would enjoy making life difficult for him. All Mackay would do was point the policeman in the right direction. Mackay would have to look for another job but that was no bad thing, at least he would be forced to do something with his life. The phone rang and Mackay picked it up.

'Tom Mackay.'

'Yes.'

'It's Nick Steadman.'

'Nick, where the hell have you been?'

'Let's just say I fell off a cliff.'

'Fell off?'

'Well, more like barged off by a local youth trying to nick my wallet.'

'Oh.' Mackay was disappointed and Steadman could hear it in his voice.

'You thought I'd been pushed off by Craven.'

'The thought had crossed my mind.'

'That's what I thought until this lad confessed. He thought he'd killed me but I was just out cold for a few days. My leg's broken but I'll make a full recovery.'

'Did this lad look anything like Craven?'

'God. I didn't think of that. Yes he did.' Mackay heard the receiver thump against the wall as Steadman put some more coins into the slot. 'That would also explain why his expensive Brief turned up so quickly from Newcastle.'

'Do you think you were pushed off?'

'Very difficult to say, you've no idea how strong the wind was. It all happened so quickly. He definitely went for my notebook and sort of shoulder barged me in the process. I couldn't be certain he tried to push me over.'

'It's suspicious nevertheless. Craven got in, you know.'

'I know. I've spoken to Roger Metcalfe. He's been leant on

from above and I've to stop digging about. There's no hard evidence anyway.' Mackay looked at the file in front of him and was tempted to contradict the journalist but he didn't.

'Listen, I just wanted to let you know that I was alright. I'm on a payphone here and the beeps have started, let's catch up when I'm back in London.'

'Bye,' said Mackay, but the line had gone dead. Mandy popped her head in the room and caught Mackay's eye.

'Inspector Steele's in reception, shall I send him up?'

'Yes,' replied Mackay, still a little dazed by Steadman's call. Was Craven telling the truth after all? The deaths in Northumberland, Peter Vassallo, Bridger, Platt… all accidents? His own attackers nothing more than hungry asylum seekers, nothing to do with Craven - the only link between them and Craven being Mackay's fevered brain. Maybe there was nothing in any of it, but Mackay didn't care. Steele's investigation would throw up enough mud to do some damage and that was all that mattered. The phone rang through from Bridger's office into the Boardroom; Mandy was not at her desk, so Mackay dialled *3 and picked it up.

'Jonathan Bridger?' said the voice.

'Yes,' replied Mackay. The caller was clearly unaware of Bridger's death. Mackay might learn something.

'My name is Richard Garcia of the Gibraltar and West Mediterranean Bank. Can I ask you a few security questions?'

'Of course,' replied Mackay, as evenly as he could manage. He quickly opened the file in front of him and turned to the 'statutory books' section where all the details of the company's directors were kept.

'Can you give me your date of birth please?'

'7th May 1945.'

'And your address?'

'Little Mill, East Chirnside, Kelso, Roxburghshire.' Now for the password, thought Mackay. Remembering Bridger's children's names, he scribbled Steven and Yvette on the post-it in front of him.'

'Can you give me the third letter of your password please?'

'E.'

'And the fourth letter?' continued Garcia.

'V' or 'T' thought Mackay. 'V,' he said softly.

'Can you repeat that please?' asked Garcia. Has he misheard me thought Mackay, or is it the wrong letter. He decided to switch children.

'T.'

'Can you repeat that please?'

'T for Tango,' said Mackay firmly. There was a long pause before the banker continued.

'And finally the last letter?'

'E for echo.'

'Thank you Mr Bridger. Mr Bridger it's about your account which you recently asked us to close.'

'Yes,' replied Mackay, feeling nervous for the first time.

'Well, following your instructions we remitted the funds into the account which you gave us at the Southern and London Bank.'

'That's right,' lied Mackay.

'Unfortunately the interest which was due on the account had not been credited at the time of the transfer Mr Bridger, I do apologise.'

'I see,' said Mackay in a much firmer tone, 'and how much is the interest?'

'£507,142.' Garcia waited for 'Bridger's' response. He'd been personally responsible for the error and he'd been charged with rectifying it at no extra cost to the bank. This had been Garcia's third mistake that year, and he prayed that 'Mr Bridger' wouldn't make a fuss and that the matter could be resolved quickly and amicably. Fortunately for Garcia, 'Mr Bridger' had no intention of making a fuss, and so Garcia was more than happy to comply with his wishes, whatever they might be. 'Mr Bridger, I'm just calling to confirm that you wish us to remit this interest to the same account at the Southern and London Bank.'

Mackay glanced at his briefcase and saw the welcome pack which he'd received from the Gibraltar and West

Mediterranean Bank via John Benady. Mackay put down the phone, pulled the documents out of his briefcase, and spread them across the desk. He quickly found the statements which showed his account details.

'Are you still there Mr Bridger?'

'Yes, I'm still here. I would like you to transfer the funds to the following account in your own branch. The account is in the name of Thomas J Mackay and the number is 0083216.'

Garcia repeated the details back to him and Mackay reconfirmed them. A flicker of suspicion had crossed the banker's mind but this had soon been suppressed. Not only would there be no complaint, but a large sum would remain with the Bank - that was a bonus.

'Thank you for your time Mr Bridger. Your account is now closed. I've already sent out confirmation of this to you last week, so I see no need to bother you with any further paperwork, unless you want it?'

'No, that won't be necessary,' said Mackay - fearful that a fresh statement outlining this recent transfer would find its way to Group Internal Audit and then the police.

'Well, thank you for your business Mr Bridger. I wish you good day.'

'Goodbye,' said Mackay weakly, and then he hung up.

Mackay glanced through the Boardroom windows across to the lift, which he saw open to reveal Inspector Steele and Sergeant Thorpe. A wave of guilt swept over him and he resolved to tell the policemen about the transfer immediately. The interest alone was hard evidence, and would no doubt help to secure a number of convictions and end several careers. He'd acted on a whim. Surely he didn't intend to steal the money, he'd simply moved the cash into his own account for safekeeping, hadn't he?

Mackay gently removed the post-its from his file and threw the fax from Avon and General casually into the bin. He closed the file and stood up as the policemen entered the Boardroom.

'Good morning Inspector.'

Printed in the United Kingdom
by Lightning Source UK Ltd.
117443UKS00001B/13-60

9 780955 427404